CIGARS !

www.barbarianspy.com

Published by BarbarianSpy, an imprint of Cyberworld Publishng
Jindalee St
Toronto NSW Australia

CIGARS!

by Shabbu

Table of Contents

Introduction

Nothing zings directly to the phallic like a well-hefted cigar. A distinctive, hard, yet soft cylindrical shape to be held, fondled, and sucked lovingly and sensuously in the mouth, providing not only strong sensations of taste, smell, and feel, but also a touch of the hedonist, a throb of risk to one's health and well-being, and red hot heat at its tip.

Habu wrote the short story *Men in Tuxedos* in April 2006. It features a scene with a cigar that I really, really like and I toyed with a cigar story of my own. The idea of putting together a jointly authored collection of cigar stories grew from there.

We both, along with a famous ex-president and his intern, find something very erotic in using the cigar as a sex toy.

But there is more to cigars than just that, there is also the smell, the wonderful aroma of quality fresh tobacco, the feel, the crinkle and smoothness of the cigar's body. The aura of wealth and elitism that expensive cigars positively drip. And the mystique that surrounds their manufacture. The image of the young native with firm sweaty thighs as cigar roller, the reader, La Lectura who reads to the often-illiterate cigar makers in the factories.

All of these aspects of the cigar rose up at us and provided inspiration for the stories in this collection.

So whether you smoke them or not, sit back and enjoy the magic of the cigar with us.

Shabbu

(Authors habu and Sabb)

Triple Magnum Nabilum

by habu

I had to turn my eyes away from the penetrating stare of Finn Bergstrum, so I took my first good look at his assistant, Nabil. "Satyr" was the first thought that entered my mind, and I almost was able to imagine two little horns above his ears there. Sharp, swarthy features with that almost sneer of a smile that was close to the edge of presumption and cruelty without losing an ability to claim interest and encouragement if challenged. Jet black hair and eyes, and that pointed goatee that accentuated the struggle between sensitivity and raw animalism. The struggle accentuated by the hand that reached out for his wine glass: Long, sensuous artist's finger, but curly black hair on the back of the hand down to his knuckles. He was giving me a proprietary look—which, of course, was his privilege. I'd been bought and paid for to be here.

I looked back at Bergstrum, embarrassed at the feeling that I was distinctly out of my depth and perhaps even out of my league, and further embarrassed that anything like this could ever embarrass me after what I'd seen in this business. When Leon had set this up and handed me the air tickets, he only said that this was a very special corporate arrangement, that I'd been very lucky to be selected, and that I should be very accommodating. From the amount on the

11

accompanying check, I decided that, indeed, I could be very accommodating. I'd flown to Zurich, checked in by prior arrangement at the Softel Hotel, and had barely slept for five hours before I was called down to the hotel's intimate and heavily masculine "gentlemen's" bar.

I had known the name Finn Bergstrum even before being handed the assignment. Who hadn't heard of him? Entrepreneur on the grand scale. Instant relief to corporations in the need of being saved and even more immediate panic in the halls of corporations rumored to have been added to his takeover lists. Reclusive, eccentric, somewhere just short of God, the tabloids said. And whispers about his sexual tastes and capabilities as well—at least in the pools in which I swam. Well, I'd just met him, and already I was trembling. This didn't normally happen to me.

He was ugly as sin, a regular gargoyle. But when I looked back at him, here in the Softel Hotel's dimly lit gentlemen's bar, I was overwhelmed by his presence and the raw power he exuded. He could have tipped me over this table right here, stripped me, and plowed me in front of all of the sedate bankers and brokers sitting around us sipping their martinis and smoking their Cuban cigars, and I would have moaned and moved my hips for him.

Craggy features, chiseled in a Mount Everest rawness and a powerful body, barely contained by a tailored silk tuxedo—heavy but obviously built for stamina and speed, the muscled presence of a bison. He filled the room; he owned the room. Strong hands the size of hubcaps and thick, gnarly fingers that set my butt a twitching.

There was no doubt why I was here, what I was supposed to do for him. This is what I did. I'd been told the bare facts of the deal.

12

He'd agreed not to take over a major U.S. corporation for certain remunerations and accommodations. I—or someone like me—was just one of the accommodations. Just for one night. All the way from New York to Zurich just for one night. What I'd found in my paycheck was more than enough to cover anything that would happen in that one night. I'd done this before—if, certainly, not on this scale.

"So, is all understood, Mr. Smith?" Bergstrum asked me, as he took a long, thin cigar out of his mouth and tapped its ash head carefully in a silver-lined wooden tray. As he did so, I noticed three silver boxes, of varying lengths and widths laying on the surface of the cocktail table between us.

His milky blue eyes, peeking out from under bushy silver-gray eyebrows, pierced me, and I looked away quickly, down to his hand, resting atop the stack of boxes. Those thick fingers. My butt twitched again. Projecting ahead. Trying to remember whether I'd heard anything specific from the rumors about his proclivities.

"Yes, certainly," I answered. "I am ticketed for an early morning flight. I assume—"

"Of course I know your flight schedule, Mr. Smith," Bergstrum said, overriding my sentence.

"Then—" I started to say, indicating that I was quite prepared to vacate the bar and get on with the evening.

"Oh, do finish your drink, Mr. Smith," Bergstrum said. "I don't think that Nabil here has finished admiring you yet. And what do you think of my assistant, Nabil, Mr. Smith? Do you find him . . . suitable?"

"Ummm. Yes, of course," I stammered. What in the hell did that mean, I wondered.

13

"Nabil, here, is my right-hand man, Mr. Smith. My hands and eyes and my ears and my . . . well, let's just say all of my appendages."

Well, Hokay, I thought. But I wasn't being paid to be confused or smart. So I turned my face toward Nabil and gave him a friendly smile. He gave me back a smart-assed look fully conveying that this night would be a double. Well, that was OK, too. That was no surprise. I couldn't shake the satyr image that pinged at my brain every time I looked at him. He wasn't tall or thin, but he was strongly built. I gauged him to be Turkish probably. Some Mediterranean blend certainly. Somewhat of a surprise set off against the hulking Norwegian. And much younger than Bergstrum. The image of the two of them fucking flashed through my mind. This was immediately followed by the vision of the two of them fucking me, and my hand trembled a little. Nabil would be nothing new, other than that satyrish puckishness about him. But Bergstrum. I just didn't know. I didn't usually lose control on the job, and he was such an ugly lump. But there was something about him that had me off balance. Those fingers. I looked at them again. Strong, thick. I couldn't help but thinking of—

"Three boxes, Mr. Smith." Bergstrum was holding up the top, squarish silver box over the table between us. "Perhaps you can give us some idea of your preference."

He flipped open the lid of the box away from me. Cigars. Five cigars, of varying brands laid out in a row, snuggled into red velvet as if they were the crown jewels—and, although I knew next to nothing about cigars, I had no doubt that these cigars were as preciously bought as crown jewels.

"Oh, no thank you," I said. "I don't smoke. Thanks anyway."

14

"Oh, these aren't for smoking, Mr. Smith." He paused and gave me a broad, friendly smile. I turned to Nabil; he gave me a leery grin.

"Let me tell you how we rate cigars," Bergstrum continued after that pregnant pause. "First, by length. All of these in this box are six inches or less in length. Sort of the standard size; but maybe a bit long . . . for a cigar." He gave me a piercing look; gauging whether I was following his meaning. I wasn't a dummy; I understood we weren't talking about cigars.

"The other rating is in girth, diameter, if you will, Mr. Smith. We call this rating ring gauge. A sixty-four ring gauge would be equal to an inch. The cigars in this box all range around fifty ring gauge. Again, a bit thick for a cigar . . . if perhaps a somewhat disappointing thickness for, well, you know."

Yes, I did know.

"But we have several cigars here," Bergstrum said, and he flashed me a broad smile.

"So," he continued, "there are some very nice cigars in this case. Indian Tabac Cameroon Legenda Gorilla—interesting name, wouldn't you say? At six inches in length and a fifty-eight ring gauge, it's quite a formidable cigar, as cigars go. Or perhaps one of my favorites; this is a La Gloria Cubana Series R., No. 6, which is slightly shorter at five and seven-eighths inches, but a bit thicker at a sixty ring gauge. Do these interest you, Mr. Smith, or would you like to see what is in the second box before noting a preference?"

"Oh, let's look in the second box," I said. Obviously I'd said the right thing, as both Bergstrum and Nabil gave me approving looks.

"You'll notice this box is longer than the first one, Mr. Smith," Bergstrum said in hushed tones. "These are the truly extraordinary gems of the cigar world." He took up the second box and flipped it open. Surprise. More cigars. Longer and thicker than those in box number one. Same silver encasing, blue velvet lining this time.

I could tell these were special to Bergstrum. He lifted them out one at a time, his hands trembling a bit. Those thick fingers lovingly handling the cigars. I could feel the heat rising in me. This was unusual for me. Bergstrum had something in him that aroused me. I had little question why he was so successful in the business world. Most probably called it charisma. I had other names for it.

"We are into the longer beauties now, Mr. Smith. Very few exist at this level. The Casa Blanca Magnum, at seven inches and a ring gauge of sixty is lovely, don't you think? Or this Padron Magnum Maduro at a full nine inches, fifty ring gauge." He was expecting me to be impressed, and I was impressed. I was being well paid to be impressed. I would have been less impressed if we were really talking about cigars, but, of course, we weren't.

"Now we could improve upon those, but we'd have to make choices." Bergstrum was continuing on. At this point I don't think he even needed me in the room. Nabil was sitting closer to Bergstrum now, and he was looking intently, worshipfully at the older man. And he had a hand on Bergstrum's inner thigh. This was obviously something of a precoital ceremony for the two of them. I said nothing. My paycheck was already banked.

"For length, you might like the Perfecxion A Giant, at nine and a quarter inches, but only a forty-seven ring gauge. And if your preference went to thickness, here's a Special Jamaican Rey Del Rey, at nine inches, but with a ring gauge of sixty. What do you think, Mr. Smith? Are these interesting to you, or should we perhaps go back to the first box?" Bergstrum's voice was rasping now. Nabil's hand had found his basket and was gently massaging it.

"No, this box is fine," I said, trying my best to match Bergstrum's rasping voice and to show him lustful eyes. He was clearly pleased. And I'll have to admit that the lustful eyes required no acting. Nabil's other hand was on my basket now, and I was showing him that I, indeed, was following along with this game.

"Then just maybe you might be interested in Orson Welles's favorite, Mr. Smith?"

"Yes, I was wondering about that one," I said in a breathy voice, having had my eye on the last cigar in the box ever since Bergstrum had opened it. If Nabil didn't stop his attentions, I might come right here in the gentlemen's bar. I could see by the way he'd tented up Bergstrum's pants that I hadn't been mistaken about those chunky fingers of his.

"This is a Casa Blanca Jeroboam," Bergstrum said, his voice full of wonder. "Orson Welles's cigar of choice. Ten inches long and a sixty-six ring gauge."

We all sat there for a moment, drinking in the size of that humongous cigar. Nabil was still stroking Bergstrum's crotch, but he had abandoned mine for his own.

"Would you like to make choices for Nabil and me, Mr. Smith?"

17

I contemplated the pickings for a few brief moments, wondering what would be most acceptable. "How about the Perfecxion A Giant for Nabil?" I said.

"And for me?" Bergstrum's eyes were slitted and his chest was heaving up and down from the attention Nabil was giving him.

"The Casa Blanca Jeroboam, of course," I said.

That had been the right answer, obviously. But I pressed on. "But what about the third box?" I asked. I could see it was longer than the other two, although much narrower.

"Ah, that would be the Triple Magnum Nabilum," Bergstrum said. "Perhaps later."

Both Bergstrum and his assistant were struggling up out of their plush club chairs at that point.

* * * *

Bergstrum's room at the Softel, or rooms, I should say, were about twelve times larger than the accommodations I had been given. And they were about four degrees plusher even though, had I not seen Bergstrum's digs, I would have assumed that I'd been given the best accommodations in the hotel.

But I didn't really see much of the room. As far as the decor went, my eyes were mainly on the edge of the canopy over Bergstrum's massive bed. I was on my back at the edge of the bed, holding my thighs up and out, and Bergstrum was hunched between them and working my ass canal with the Perfecxion A. Giant cigar I'd selected for Nabil, while Nabil was over to the side, clearly in my vision, stripping down.

The cigar was somewhat of a surprise; the foreplay down in the gentlemen's bar hadn't been as symbolic as I had imagined it would be. I really was being fucked by an expensive nine and a half-inch cigar. But in my line of business and at the prices I commanded, this wasn't as surprising as some other moments in my life had been.

Nabil was much more of a surprise. The satyr impression held true. His dark-skinned well-muscled torso was smooth skin down to the waist, with the exception of patches of black curly hair around his ring-pierced nipples, but when he stripped his tuxedo pants off, I could hardly tell he'd done so. From the waist down, he was covered in thick, curly black hair that looked almost like a pelt. His forearms were equally hirsute. If he'd had cloven feet, I would have sworn he was a true satyr. As it was he certainly was horse hung.

Leaving the Perfecxion A Giant buried in my ass, Bergstrum moved back to the other side of me from where Nabil had stripped and sank into a chair, still well within my line of vision. Nabil cantered up to him and Bergstrum took Nabil's cock in his mouth and worked it up. After only a few moments, however, Nabil walked back over to me and retrieved the cigar. He went to a side table, put the cigar in his mouth, struck a match to the tip of the cigar, and took a few puffs. Then he returned to Bergstrum, stuck the cigar in Bergstrum's mouth, sank down to his knees between Bergstrum's thighs, unzipped the hulking Norwegian's tux fly, and fed on the huge piece of meat he found there. Bergstrum let his head loll back on the top of the chair and hummed and puffed on the cigar. After a bit, he groaned and lurched, and I could tell he had come.

He picked up box number two from a table beside the chair and handed Nabil the Casa Blanca Jeroboam cigar. Nabil approached me between my now relaxed legs, lifted my legs up and out, and made clear I was to hold my own legs up, which I did—ever mindful of what

19

I was being paid for this—while he fucked me with the thicker and longer Casa Blanca Jeroboam.

Bergstrum sat in his chair, legs thrown out, cigar puffing, and a beefy hand stroking his own cock back to life as he watched Nabil slowly, and inventively, work my ass canal with the Casa Blanca Jeroboam. At length, Bergstrum gave a hoarse cough, lurched up from his chair, and joined Nabil between my legs. He forced the wet end of the Perfecxion alongside the Casa Blanca Jeroboam inside me, and I now was being fucked more fully and quite deeply with two counterpistoning cylinders of expensive tobacco. Nabil was working my nipples with his free hand, and Bergstrum was stroking my cock. At the same time, they were doing a good lip lock on each other. Those strong, beefy fingers of Bergstrum's wrapped around my cock and stroking it. Oh, Gawd. And they continued this until I ejaculated.

Then it was Bergstrum back in his chair, with Nabil kneeling between his thighs and giving him another blow job.

"You asked about the third box, Mr. Smith," Bergstrum called over to me. "About the Triple Magnum Nabilum."

"Umm, umm," I replied. Still mellow after my meltdown.

He lifted and opened the third box, which had been lying under box number two on the table. He turned and showed me the contents of the box.

Surprise. Yet another cigar. But, carumba, what a cigar.

"Ten and a half inches long, 120 ring gauge. Almost not big enough to get in my mouth, Mr. Smith. I have these made specially for me. And do you know where the name came from, Mr. Smith?"

"Umm, umm," I repeated.

"Triple Magnum Nabilum, Mr. Smith. Nabilum. From Nabil, Mr. Smith. Our own Nabil here provided the specifications for them, Mr. Smith."

"Umm, umm," I managed.

"And now I smoke this, Mr. Smith . . . while you smoke Nabil."

Oh.

While I watched Bergstrum lean back in his chair, legs thrown out, mouth puffing his huge Triple Magum Nabilum, and his hand stroking his cock, he watched Nabil fuck me with his ten-and a half-inch long, two-inch-in-diameter cock through much of the rest of the night.

Despite all of my professional training, I cried out at the first entry, and moaned and groaned and bunched up clumps of satin bedspread in my fists and did what I could not to bite off my tongue as a sneering satyr of prodigious proportions and inhuman staying power fucked me to his completion. The satyr image kept floating up, as our hips swung back and forth, my legs wrapped around his waist and my hands gripping the heavy pelting of his bulbous buttocks and heavily muscled thighs. I had been trained to please a man, and I could tell that Nabil was beside himself with lust to be drawn as far as he could inside me and to explore every nook and cranny of my channel. As he was about to pull out of me for his first shooting, I contracted my canal closely around his sword and held him inside me, riding his pelvis hard as he twitched and then lurched again and again and again. A series of little cries from the direction of Bergstrum's chair gave evidence that he was joining us in release.

After ejaculating, Nabil brought his mouth down onto my nipples and ravished them while he stroked me to another flowing. Then he turned me belly down on the bed and fucked me again to ejaculation and then turned me and dug in even deeper and stretched me even wider, with Bergstrum puffing on his Triple Magnum Nabilum and coming in consort with Nabil's spoutings as if they practiced this every night.

On the plane trip home the next morning, as the soreness of my body and my inability to close my legs made me ever grateful for the first class ticket, my one regret was that Bergstrum hadn't fucked me. I left aching for that. That was the power he had.

Maybe next time.

Getting It All

by Sabb

The air conditioner rattled and hummed in the tropical air, but inside the office at the top of the iron staircase, it felt as if it was doing nothing but stirring the humidity around. If there was any coolness, it came more from the big ceiling fan that whirled and clacked in the center of the ceiling.

Luca sat back in his office chair under the fan and smiled as he wiped sweat from his forehead and his muscular, almost hairless chest with a hand towel. He was wearing only a pair of loose, lightweight cotton shorts. The longer he stayed in Africa the less he wore. Now, after five months of running his employer, Oscar Riddleman's, tobacco-processing factory in Cameroon, he would have to go completely naked if he wanted to wear less. And at home he did, but this was work.

Towel in hand Luca got up and looked out of the side window, seeing below him the busy floor of the open-sided factory shed where the young men and women were working rolling cigars. From above most of them looked as if they were barely more than children. And seated as they were in rows at long benches, bent over their work, with their fingers flying over the tobacco leaves they were wrapping, they might have been students studying hard. So much for the rolling of cigars against the sweaty thighs of muscular young black men, he thought, remembering his first meeting with Riddleman with a smile.

As soon as they met, Luca had a good idea that his potential employer, Oscar Riddleman, was interested in more than his knowledge of tobacco processing and cigar manufacture, even though that was extensive, or his management skills.

Sure Luca knew cigars like few other men did, and his were very unusual management skills, but still there was something in Riddleman's eyes that said even more was wanted. Well, Luca had no objection to that. Riddleman was a powerful and well-built man who liked control and wealth, and giving men like him what they wanted had never hurt Luca. In fact, it had helped him to climb from being a lazy, good-looking student in high school to being quite a wealthy man in his own right. If it had seen him escaping over back roads in the dead of night from several small South American countries, well, such was life. It had got him here, and with this new job he might end up doing for Riddleman, in Africa, he would become even richer.

"So you don't object to something that is downright illegal then," Riddleman asked twirling a cigar between his fingers as he stood leaning on the mantle of the marble fireplace in the ground floor drawing room of his home.

"Shall we say, I'm versatile?" Luca replied giving Riddleman a bedroom smile.

Legal was a word that didn't really mean much to Luca, who did whatever seemed like a good way to make money and get him what he wanted from life. But he had always been fascinated by tobacco and cigars, and he had some good experience in the associated business of cigarette-tobacco selection and grading.

"Do you think you can handle the machinery? This is Africa. The locals in the factory wont have a clue, and there's no service guy waiting up the road on the end of the phone to help you."

"I will manage," Luca replied, dropping the bedroom look. He had taken a few bad steps in his time and had learnt to be resourceful. He did whatever it took to survive and prosper. "In Panama I kept the cigar machines going for six months during the trouble. I can be very resourceful, Oscar. I have worked in many places that are not peaceful and quiet like this Virginia of yours, and where the workers hardly know what electricity is, let alone machinery."

"That's why you are here, Luca," Riddleman said looking at him and moving over to sit in the chair opposite the one Luca was sprawled back in. "I have asked around," he added.

Luca wondered who he had been talking to but decided thinking about it was pointless.

"What I can do is useless if your contacts are not good," he responded instead, annoyed to be the only one having to prove anything. "This money you say we will make, is going to depend on you having good contacts, and the police and customs being taken care of."

"Don't trouble yourself, Luca. That side is dealt with. I can sell whatever my factory can make with you running it," Riddleman said firmly.

Now Riddleman was sitting opposite Luca, leaning back in his overstuffed leather chair with his legs spread wide, and he asked him,

"So you think you can give me whatever I want?" while twisting a fresh cigar between his lips to wet the end of it.

"I know I can," Luca had replied, smiling, and then he was kneeling between Riddleman's spread thighs and reaching for his zipper.

"Not so fast boy," Riddleman said, pushing Luca back, "Not so fast. This business may not be completely legal, but I still want high-quality products. Good cigars and a high-quality cigarette that 80 percent of our customers won't be able to pick from the real thing. And the rest won't be sure about. I want to be in this business for a while Luca, not ten minutes."

"Of course. We both want that," Luca replied, suddenly uncertain of what was expected of him.

"Whatever else I want from you, first of all I want to know that you really do know how to produce a decent cigar. And to produce a decent cigar you need to know a decent cigar when you pick it up and sniff it," Riddleman said, leaning forward and holding the cigar he had been sucking on under Lucas nose and rolling it between his thumb and forefinger, making it crackle.

Luca sniffed at it, annoyed, "It smells genuine to me," he said, "Not the absolute best, but real Cuban. Hand rolled. You can see that."

Instead of settling back into his overstuffed club chair to smoke his cigar, Riddleman stood up, almost between Luca's thighs, and said, "That was easy. Now I think we will take a little walk."

Luca joined him as he strode a short distance down the wood-paneled hallway of Mystrelle, the historic Virginian plantation house that Riddleman had recently acquired and was now living in. Part way along he opened one of the heavy paneled doors and held it wide for Luca to pass him, then followed him inside and closed it. The room was dry and cool and dark—dimly lit and lined with dark timber. Riddleman opened a panel, and Luca realized that around the walls were dozens of small paneled cupboard doors. But they were not ordinary cupboards; each one was a small humidor, and inside each humidor rested several cigars.

"So," Riddleman said, "Let's try a test, shall we?" And he took a cigar from the open cupboard and passed it to Luca, who took it carefully between his thumb and forefinger and examined it, then brought it to his nose to roll and sniff.

"Santa Damiana," Luca said with assurance, he'd worked in the Dominican Republic, "Delicate flavor."

Riddleman took the cigar back and, putting it away, opened another door and gave Luca a longer and thicker cigar.

This time Luca frowned. "Ha, a good one, a Big Butt. Not as good as the one in your mouth now. Maduro, Pennsylvanian wrapper."

"So, you really do know your stuff," Riddleman said, smiling broadly. "I see us getting along fine together. But I wonder what you will make of this one," he said, opening yet another humidor cupboard and taking out a huge bullet-shaped cigar. "This one has just come in. Rolled on the sweaty thighs of muscular young men." He said, smiling and laughing as he handed it over.

"Phew," Luca said, wrinkling his nose. "Good leaf and not badly made, yes, from Africa, Cameroon, I think. But so big and thick, humph, who could smoke it, and the smell—yeow, it is almost animal. It is not the tobacco." He looked at Riddleman suspiciously.

"Ah, but what is the smell?" Riddleman asked, his eyes hooded now as if he were in heat.

Luca frowned and sniffed again, closing his eyes. Then he laughed.

"It is a cigar for fun," he said, feeling his cock twitch, and making a back and forth movement with the eight-inch-long, more-than-inch-and-a-half-thick cigar. "They have amused themselves in the factory with this one."

"Hmmm," Riddleman hummed, waving the cigar away as Luca tried to hand it back to him. "You may like to know it comes from the factory you may soon be managing. And what was fucked with it?" Riddleman asked in a husky voice.

"The ass," Luca replied in a low voice, letting Riddleman lock eyes with him as the cigar was finally passed back to him.

"And how else do you think you can satisfy me?" Riddleman asked. "You obviously know enough to make sure we produce a good cigar, and hopefully a good enough cigarette to fool most men, but what else can you do for me?" He asked, holding the ass-scented cigar in front of him and still fixing Luca with his hooded eyes.

Luca felt the heat rise up in his body, like a physical surge racing through him, and moved in and kissed Riddleman on the mouth. Then he hesitated a moment, not entirely sure how to go on, because Riddleman stood there, immobile, holding the cigar. Then Luca started to unbutton his own shirt. He was in a casual shirt and pants, because this had been an informal interview. No human resources manager would have been satisfied with the selection procedure Riddleman used, and Luca hadn't felt he needed to look like an accountant when he dressed for the meeting.

Now Luca undressed as if he were performing a striptease to some unheard music, and he was more than aroused himself by the setting, by the thick, used cigar, and the lustful look in Riddleman's half-closed eyes. He fixed his eyes on the big cigar, sure now that Riddleman knew exactly what he wanted to do with it and that he, Luca, had guessed exactly what that was. And he was interested. He liked to be dominated like this sometimes. And Riddleman was a man who could dominate.

Luca's cock sprang up against his flat belly as he removed his briefs, and he stood there naked, as he wrapped one hand about his erection and stroked himself and pinched his nipples and stroked his belly before cupping his balls in his other hand. But as he was getting ready to turn around, Riddleman extended the cigar and pressed it to Luca's lips, and Luca laughed silently as he opened up to allow it into this mouth. Then he closed his lips and made love to the big, fat, smooth-skinned cigar with his tongue and cheeks, wetting it down and caressing it, deep throating the slick column of tobacco as Riddleman fucked it in and out of Luca's mouth.

Luca's eyes were locked on Riddleman's as he made love to the cigar in his mouth and stroked his own cock, though he wanted to be stroking Riddleman's cock. Wanted to be taken. The big man's free hand was flicking over his new employee's chest and squeezing Luca's nipples and then ran down to join Luca's hand stroking his cock before it descended to his balls and squeezed them. Luca opened his mouth and cried out, as his cock spouted cum up onto Riddleman's shirt and up his own belly.

When the cigar was finally withdrawn from his mouth, well soaked in saliva, Luca and Riddleman both seemed to shudder in an ecstasy of shared heat, and Luca turned and bent over, reaching back and parting his firm round butt cheeks, to open his crack and present his hole to Riddleman.

Luca was happy to let Riddleman believe he owned his new employee, his new factory manager, because right then in the humidor-lined room, he almost did.

Luca's breathing was jerky as the wet cigar was pressed to his rim and moved around it, rimming him with the damp, tightly rolled end of the column of tobacco. His hole twitched wildly, opening up, wanting Riddleman to force the thick cigar in. Then the cigar was being pushed in, lubricated by its saliva coating. His own spit and Riddleman's, helping it move into his well-used channel.

Luca couldn't suppress his moan of pleasure as it dragged along his walls on its slightly painful entry. And as it was rotated and fucked into him, he bucked and begged as eagerly for it to go deeper and harder as he would for any big cock that might be filling him. Maybe even more, as knowing it was a cigar already worked inside the passage of at least one of the young men in the factory he was going to be taking over, aroused him even more.

Only when the cigar had opened him fully was it withdrawn, and Luca still held his cheeks apart in anticipation, though his own cock ached for some attention. Riddleman was not as thick as the cigar had been, but his full length could enter Luca, burying itself deep until his mass of dark pubic hair was crushed against the Latin's skin, and Luca groaned as the big man drove his hard tool into him. When Riddleman was pumping him hard and deep, Luca finally reached for his own cock and stroked it.

But Riddleman had other ideas and wanted control, and taking hold of Luca's wrists, jerked on his arms, up and back, pulling Luca back to him as he thrust deep, getting even more depth to his fucking as Luca felt pain in his arms and a deep fullness and real possession. Then Riddleman had pulled out, his big fat cock slurping, and with both men panting, had pushed Luca to one of the walls and turned him around facing him, and had him hike his legs up around his hips and settled him back onto his cock.

Luca embraced Riddleman as he lowered himself down ad lifted himself up fucking himself, rubbing his own throbbing tool up against the big man's slightly bulging belly, moaning and opening his mouth for a kiss. Riddleman dug his tongue into Luca's mouth and explored it briefly.

Then Riddleman was pushing Luca's chest back and moving away from the dark wood-paneled wall. Luca suddenly lost his grip and his head and arms fell back to the floor, Riddleman's big, surprisingly strong hands gripping his hips, the fingers digging in until Luca had himself balanced on his shoulders, Then Riddleman fucked down into him, and as Luca looked up his belly, he saw a cigar and screamed out as Riddleman lay the tobacco pole against the top of his cock. Luca was almost sobbing with relief as he saw it was the Cuban cigar Riddleman had been mouthing earlier, not the African monster, that was now pressing to the top of Riddleman's own cock. A cock pulled back in Luca's hole so that the tip of the cigar could work its way in the first small distance. Luca arched and moaned and spread his thighs as wide as he could, crying out at the rough stretching that the thick cock and the premium cigar were giving him, and moaning loudly as Riddleman expertly worked the two hard tools together in his stretched passage, in a wild plowing that was over too soon in a flooding creaming of Luca's guts.

Then a hand encased Luca's throbbing cock and squeezed and rubbed his cap and in a wild spasm, he spouted cum up onto Riddleman's chest and chin, then spouted another load as his cock was milked again. Totally spent, Luca's legs let go and he slid to the floor, looking up at Riddleman, who stood between his tangled legs and looked down at him with a satisfied smile on his face.

It was then, while observing Riddleman's expression as he looked down on him, with his cum dribbling from his ass, that Luca decided he didn't like Riddleman and was going to see how much money he could screw out of him. And Luca knew almost as much about screwing money out of wealthy men as he did about cigars.

* * * *

Those Luca saw working below him as he looked out over the cigar factory through his office window were mostly bone and ropy sinews. Big heads and undernourished, with flashing white teeth. He was no philanthropist, but he knew the factory workers were better off than most of the others in their villages, than most in Cameroon, in fact, and work in the factory was eagerly sought.

Then Luca walked to the other side of his office and looked out on the other part of the factory. The part that he had spent the time since his arrival setting up for Riddleman. It was smaller, but the floor was concrete and fully enclosed, and it was filled with modern cigarette making machines, with several young men working in the hot, steamy conditions, watching the machines as they spun out hundreds of thousands of cigarettes each day. They were being wrapped in fine white paper with a tan patterned band below a strip of type that said

Marlboro on it and packed in the familiar red and white packet. And, in fact, the quality of the cigarettes Luca knew was very good. They were good enough to be accepted in most places in place of the real thing and even went to the Canary Islands and Spain.

This part of the factory was where the brightest and best workers were employed, and here the young men were more filled out. As he watched, one man walked up the corridor between the two rows of machines, and his hips moved in a way that showed off his full-rounded butt. Luca smiled, sure that Misoni was hoping he, Luca, was watching him.

Luca flipped the intercom switch on the phone on his desk. "Misoni" was all he said.

Several youths looked up at the window, or at Misoni, and grinned as the young black man made his way up the metal staircase, which clanged with each step, telling Luca when he had arrived in the outer office where Margaret, Luca's secretary sat. She knew better than to ask any questions, or to gossip, and just looked down her nose at Misoni, the latest young man to be making the climb, barely looking up from her computer screen as the young man opened Luca's office door and stepped through.

The young man's mouth was split in a gleaming white smile, and he was dropping his shorts and grasping his already-engorging dick as the door closed behind him. Luca had also shed his shorts and pushed his chair away from his desk, so he was sitting in plain view of the door, with his own heavily veined erection in his fist and a smile on his face.

Misoni dropped to his knees between Luca's spread thighs and, holding his bosses meaty tool steady, the young African took the

33

huge pole into his mouth, his experience with sucking showing in how quickly he was deep throating its full length. Luca growled in response and took hold of the black man's hair as his black curly head bobbed up and down over Luca's lap, his cock sliding in and out of Misoni's tight lips and sinking into his even tighter throat. What he lacked in sophisticated technique Misoni more than made up for in enthusiasm and his ability to take it all.

Luca fucked the ready mouth for a while, moving his tool about inside the soft cavern as Misoni worked his tongue about, eagerly slobbering and sucking on what he was being fed. Then when he was ready, Luca pulled himself out of Misoni's mouth and pulled the young man up and turned him around and lay him across his desk on his stomach

From his desk drawer Luca pulled out the lubricant and condoms and fingered the gel roughly into Misoni's hole, enjoying the young man's squirming and yelping. When Luca was done with Misoni's passage, he crowned himself and sat back, and the young African came up and lowered himself onto Luca's throbbing pole, Luca guiding his cap to Misoni's hole and letting him impale himself slowly on its full length.

Luca groaned at the slow encasing of his tool by the experienced bottom settling down on him.

"Yes. Nice and tight," He moaned and pulled Misoni down hard.

"Oh boss. Oh boss. You is so big," Misoni squealed.

"Ha," Luca gasped, fully encased and starting to lift Misoni's hips, "Tell me, I am the best fucking boss you have ever had?"

"You are the best fucking, fucking boss I have ever had, boss," Misoni cried out as he lifted himself up along the rod buried inside him, and then settled down on it again. "Yes boss, you are sure the best fucking boss," he sighed as he lifted his butt again, wriggling as he settled back, moving Luca's long cock inside him, so it was rubbing new places on its journey up and up.

There were voices outside briefly, talking English, and then a giant of a black man opened the office door, stepped inside, and closed it, and Luca looked up into the face of Ahmadou, the locally based American agent for the cigarette manufacturing equipment. The new arrival already had his pants unzipped and his big fat cock out, stroking the dark rod to hardness.

"How long have you been watching?" Luca asked, with a lazy laugh, his cock growing even longer inside the youth he was fucking at the idea of the huge black man watching through one of the windows as he plowed Misoni

"Long enough to enjoy it and to be ready to join you," Ahmadou replied in perfect English with an American accent.

Ahmadou threw a folder onto the desk and dropped his pants and briefs, kicking them off as he walked over to join the two men. Misoni was pushed forward over Luca's desk and his boss moved with him, never losing his depth in the young man in his lap. Ahmadou then rolled the office chair away from behind them and moved in, pushing Luca forward further over the back of the youth under him so his hole was conveniently positioned. Adding spit to his fingers, Ahmadou dug two of them into the puckered hole between the white ass cheeks, as Luca bit down on Misoni's neck and shoulders to stifle his yelps.

Then Ahmadou rummaged in the condom drawer, quickly covered his pole, and was poking his mushroom cap at Luca's hole as the white man wriggled his ass and widened his legs to open himself and ease the pain of Ahmadou's rough entry.

Ahmadou watched as his black dick slid into the hole between the white mounds of Luca's cheeks and then was plowing Luca hard and deep, while Luca managed to do shallow pumps into Misoni's ass. It was a wonderful sight, Ahmadou thought, as he looked down at the almost white body caught between the black "bread" of the sandwich the three of them made. He hummed happily as he watched his big black tool work in and out of Luca's pale white ass, seeing below Luca's balls and the base of his cock the black ass of Misoni, with the light cock slipping in and out of his tight hole.

"What a sight," Ahmadou murmured, "White meat in the sandwich. Oh baby."

The two foreigners came together; Ahmadou felt his balls tighten and was pounding Luca's ass when he saw Luca's balls move and his cock twitch as it deposited its seed in the condom deep inside Misoni. Then Luca felt Ahmadou pull out, heard the slap of the rubber coming off, and felt cum shoot over his back to the gasps and pants of the big American. The young African, Misoni, only came after the two men had come off him and he was able to reach for his own tool and stroke it to completion.

"Ahh, you young men," Ahmadou said, laughing as Misoni's eyes rolled and his jizm shot across the floor. "Now go back to work" he added, and the young man grabbed his clothes and pulled on his shorts and T-shirt and was out of the door in seconds. Ahmadou had been known to turn nasty when he wasn't obeyed.

"So, you go to America to see Riddleman?" Ahmadou said to the spent Luca once the youth was gone.

"Yes. Riddleman's invitation to come and discuss progress was very convenient," Luca replied, lying back on the desk and playing with his nipples, wondering if he could get the black giant interested in another round. He was also reminded of Riddleman's indication that there might be some more satisfying private entertainment available during Luca's visit.

"So our plans are going well?" Ahmadou said smiling broadly.

Luca shrugged and reached for Ahmadou's arms and pulled himself up, seeing that, unfortunately, the American was all business. "You have got the paperwork?" he asked, "All official, and signed by the president?"

"Of course. He is a great friend of Riddleman, but I am also his good friend," he laughed, "And as this is only for the disposition of his friend Riddleman's Cameroon businesses if he dies in debt to us, Mr. President was willing to sign the papers for the fee we offered, and here are your copies," said Ahmadou, pulling some documents from the folder he had brought in.

"And we can prove he owes us money," Luca said, opening a manila folder containing details of the cigarette machine purchases and some extra items Riddleman had never ordered from Ahmadou, or paid for, but which sat downstairs in the factory. "Well, my plans are all in order too," Luca said. And he went into a deep kiss with the African. "Yes. In a week Riddleman will be gone, very sad, and there will be no doubts the factory, the plantations, the mansion in Douala, the cash, all of it, are ours. In a week."

Ahmadou looked at Luca with hooded eyes, and Luca knew that the well-connected African-American probably had little intention of letting him, Luca, enjoy any of it for long.

When Ahmadou left, Luca pulled open the lower drawer of his desk, and, taking the papers Ahmadou had left, he put them together with the ones he already had and put them all into a large envelope.

"Unfortunately, my good friend Ahmadou," Luca said to the empty room, as he tapped the envelope, "I have already sold the plantations and the factory to the Chinese state tobacco company, which has more influence with the government here than either you or Riddleman do. Once I am in the states and Riddleman is gone, the deal will be finalized to my great advantage, and I will not have to return to this sweaty dump again."

Luca sat there gazing into the future, a future where he never needed to work for anyone else again.

"But I'll miss the fucks," he added wistfully, thinking of Ahmadou's big meaty cock and the obligingly eager young African workers he had enjoyed for the last few months.

Men in Tuxedos

by habu

"Man, don't you ever give up?" Dave asked in exasperation, removing Zane's hand from his basket and rising from the sofa and moving over to a stool by the bar.

"No, Dave, I never give up. Not when there's something I want like I want you."

"I should have known when you brought me up here and offered me all of that fine liquor. You just wanted to get me drunk and have your way with me, didn't you?"

"Yes, that was the general idea," Zane said dryly, a smile of perseverance on his lips. "What's the problem? You don't find me attractive?"

"Yeah, you're plenty attractive all right, Zane," Dave said, with a glint of defiance in his eye. "And well you know it to. I just don't open my legs for anyone who says he wants me."

"You sure open them for Karl," Zane retorted, the smile just as sparkly as before.

"Karl's different," Dave said.

"Right. Karl has money and position and is a proper sugar daddy. Karl can get you some place. You know what that kind of arrangement is called, don't you?"

"Yeah, that's called good old American barter trade," Dave shot back. "Quality goods for quality services. And I see no reason for you or anyone else to look down your nose at it."

"Oh, I'm not," Zane answered calmly. "Believe me, I've been there myself."

"Excuse me?" Dave said, surprised and intrigued now. "You of the Ivy League education and good Wall Street job?"

"Right," Zane responded, getting a glint of an opening here. Maybe if Dave saw him on equal footing he'd come across with what Zane was after. Maybe the evening wouldn't be yet another loss in this long-term battle to win Dave.

"So, what do you know of what a guy's got to do to make it in this town?" Dave challenged.

"I didn't come from money, Dave," Zane shot back. "I know it looks like I did from this apartment and from my education, but I earned my education on my back—just like you are doing with Karl."

"What do you mean?" Suddenly all of Dave's antennae were up. He was suddenly very interested in what Dave was saying.

"I put myself through school by working for a hard-core call boy service," Zane revealed. "I came to this lifestyle through hard work."

Dave was all interest now, and he returned to the sofa and started pelting Zane with questions. He took a couple of swigs of scotch from the generous portion Zane had poured out for him and settled back in the sofa cushions. He didn't even seem to mind when Zane put a hand on his thigh and started working it up his leg—or if he noticed, he didn't seem to mind. He only wanted to hear the gory details of Zane's past now.

"And what was your strangest assignment?" Dave asked Zane at the end of a flurry of other questions that Zane had dutifully responded to. "I mean, can you remember any? There must have been some."

Zane chewed on that one briefly—but only briefly, because he didn't want Dave to zero in on his hand, which now was on Dave's bare belly, under the hem of his shirt. His other arm was snaked around Dave's shoulder.

"Hmmm, let's see. That might have been the night of the men in the tuxedos."

"The men in the tuxedos?" Dave was all ears.

"Yes. As the night was starting out, I knew I was in for a workout, because the caller had specified he wanted someone experienced with men and had authorized for the full unlimited service for a four-hour period. That usually meant multiple ass work, although it's true that some out-of-town hicks just didn't realize what the various options were and had more money than brains when they set up a session.

"The address I was given was for a large, but nondescript brownstone, up on 57th Street, near Central Park. A polished brass plate by the doorbell simply stated that I was at some club, Hedgewood or Hedgeneck, or something like that. I later assumed that it was one of those old-world highly exclusive men's clubs that had existed for a couple of centuries without catching the public eye.

"I was met at the door by the epitome of a butler type who told me to follow him toward the back of the house. Outside a double oaken door set in a whole hallway of polished oaken paneling carpeted with an Oriental rug in vibrant colors, he told me to strip entirely and

41

to leave my clothes folded on a Chippendale arm chair that was located next to the door. I did so, and then he knocked twice on the door, opened it, and ushered me into the room.

"I was in some sort of club room. Leather-upholstered arm chairs sitting on a huge Oriental carpet in the middle of a wood-paneled room with glass-fronted shelves of books on three walls and on the third wall a fireplace flanked by French doors that apparently led to garden at the rear of the building. At the opposite end of the room from the fireplace was a large mahogany desk with a leather top. The arm chairs were arranged in a circle in the center of the room, facing each other, with a clear space out in the center. There were six chairs, each with a little cigarette table beside it and a brass floor lamp behind it. All of the lamp shades were turned up so that they functioned as spotlights trained on the circle in front the chairs. Each of the chairs was occupied by a man in a tuxedo. All of the men were fairly young—none older than his mid forties—and all had the air of pampering to a high gloss and well-toned physiques and of highly successful position. They had brandy snifters in their manicured and bejeweled hands, and each was smoking a cigar. The air was cloudy with the smell of premium Cuban cigar smoke."

"Come to the center of the room, please, son," a strong, willful voice commanded me from the depths of the cigar smoke cloud. I did as I was bade.

"Turn, please. Turn completely around. Slowly please. Again please. Stand straight and tall, please. You have nothing to be ashamed of." I slowly turned a few times, obviously letting them all see what they were paying for, for whatever purpose—which I had yet to discern.

42

"Now masturbate for us, please. To completion. Do not worry about where it goes." The same commanding voice. From the intensity of the light directed from the lamps and the thickness of the cigar smoke, I could not be sure which tuxedo had spoken.

"Excuse me?" I asked. In shock more at the incongruity of the setting than at the request itself. I had known it would be a performance evening for me. They had paid dearly for it. This assignment would carry me nearly a month at school all by itself.

"Masturbate, please. And do it slowly and don't hold back on your expression and response, please."

"So, I did as they asked. I had been trained what to do with this sort of request, but I had always assumed it would be something involved in a one-on-one situation."

"I was progressing pretty well, when I sensed movement in the room behind me, and I heard the rustle of rich material close behind me and hot breath on my neck. I looked down, and an arm came around me from behind. It was clothed in luxurious black material. White starched cuffs showed at the wrist, with gold nugget cuff links. An elegant, manicured hand with a signet ring wrapped itself around my engorged cock after brushing my hand away.

"Another black-clad figure was now at the other side of me. I turned enough to see the brilliant white shirt front and the satiny lapel on the tuxedo. The hand of this figure also went to my cock, and the two tuxedos worked my cock in unison and rubbed their expensive evening suits against my bare arms.

"Another figure, a commanding figure, probably the source of the voice that had given me direction, appeared through the cloud of smoke before me. He was sucking on a long cigar and giving me a very

43

intense look. He was perhaps the oldest of the men present. Very handsome, with strong facile features and intense black eyes. The light was reflecting off the diamond studs cascading down the front of his perfectly cut tuxedo. I remember thinking that one of those studs alone would be enough to get me out of the business and cover the rest of my college. He gave me a grin, almost a leer, and then he turned the cigar in his mouth, took it out, and pressed it between my lips. It was moist from his saliva. He rotated it in my mouth, adding my saliva to his, and then he grinned again and moved out of my line of vision.

"He obviously had moved to behind me, because I felt hands pulling my butt cheeks apart—in fact I found hands everywhere on my thighs and belly and nipples, in addition to the two that were stroking my cock—and I bowed my legs outward as I felt the moist end of the cigar working its way into my ass.

"The heel of a hand came up under my chin, the fingers covering my lower jaw and the thumb pushing its way into my mouth, obviously wanting me to give suck, which I did. Meanwhile, the two hands were still stroking my cock, the fingers of both of my hands were being taken into mouths and sucked, and that cigar was being rotated in my ass, being screwed in deeper and deeper and rotated around.

"I was panting heavily at the attention, the feeling of being shrouded in elegant black satin and silks and white starched shirts, flashing studs, and heavy cigar smoke. Aroused by the contrast of my being completely naked and vulnerable and being stroked and invaded everywhere by fully and elegantly clothed men.

"The cigar twisted out of my ass, and the commanding figure came back around to close in front of me. He gave me that leering, possessive smile, and then he put the cigar back in his mouth and twisted it. His eyes lit up with a mischievous gleam, and I felt a strong hand cupping my balls, coming in under the stroking hands of other tuxedos, and he squeezed hard. I threw my head up in a primeval scream of pain and surprise and release to the ceiling, jerking my mouth away from the thumb I was sucking, and shot a strong fountain of semen I know not where.

"The teeming mass of black silk and satin took my ejaculation as some sort of sign, because I was lifted and carried by a bevy of tuxedos over to the leather-topped mahogany desk. At first I was bent over that on my belly. Once again hands pulled my cheeks wide. Then fingers, slippery with lubrication, of different sizes, invaded me, pulling my well-used hole wide. The cigar again now, soggy with lubricant, entering between the fingers and twirling and screwing into me. I was panting and moaning now. The cigar twirled out, but the three fingers of different sizes remained, pulling me, stretching my hole wide. I arched my back, as a thicker, throbbing object, a cock, slid in between the fingers. The fingers pulled out as the cock plowed in, deeper, deeper, deeper. And then it started a furious rhythmic slapping back and forth into me as I counterthrusted my hips back to it until I heard a deep-throated cry and felt my insides being creamed. A second cock replaced the first and I was fucked vigorously and deeply from the rear by one cock while another tuxedoed figure on the other side of the desk pushed another cock into my mouth. At no time did I see man flesh during the whole ritual. Cocks were buried in my ass and mouth, but the tuxedos remained fully in place otherwise.

"I was completely naked, being fully possessed by six elegant tuxedos, heavy, hard, virile cocks invading me from within the folds of the rich material, but never seen.

"When the first set of tuxedos had spent their seed in either end of me, I was turned on my back and fucked repeatedly in succession, each man obviously taking more than one turn at me, with two tuxedos holding my arms out and two more spread-eagling my legs.

"As something of a finale, I was lifted off the desk and a tuxedo came in under me and settled me on his black silk lap, his cock buried in my ass, and another tuxedo came in at me from the front and penetrated me with his member as well. The most athletic of the tuxedos was hunched on top of the desk, black silk pant legs against my naked chest and me deep-throating his cock, chaffing my chin and cheeks on the zipper of the only slightly parted fly.

"I found myself draped, naked and covered with repeated semen of six men, over the top of the desk, moaning my elegant defilement, trying to concentrate on the fee I had earned for the evening. When I was able, I pulled myself up to a sitting position. The six chairs once more were occupied by six sedately and richly clad gentlemen sipping their brandy and puffing their cigars and looking very satiated and pleased with themselves.

"The commanding voice then thanked me for my time and told me I was to leave. I dragged myself out into the hall, dressed with my aching muscles feeling every move, and received a generous tip from the butler before I was shown to the door."

When Zane had finished this story, the room was silent for the longest moment except for the heavy panting coming from a still-mesmerized Dave. Zane could feel the young man trembling as well without the folds of his arms.

"Yes, I think that might have been my strangest assignment," Zane said finally, marking closure to his tale.

"Wow." That seemed to be all Dave could say at the moment. And Zane didn't want to break the moment. While he had been telling Dave this story, Dave had been so mesmerized that he didn't seem to realize that Zane had gotten his pants unzipped, had the young man's very nice cock out, and was slowly stroking him.

"So, what do you think?" Zane finally said, needing to either progress or be forced to retreat.

A few more moments of silence except for Dave's soft moaning and sighing and the rustle of the cheap cotton material of his pants in its rhythmic countermovement to Zane's slow stroking motion.

"You wouldn't . . . You wouldn't happen to own a tuxedo?" Dave asked in a hoarse, struggled whisper.

"Why, yes. Yes I do. I think I can find a box of fine Cuban cigars too," Zane said just before Dave lifted his lips to Zane's and sank into a deep, passionate, moaning kiss.

Keeping the Staff Happy

by Sabb

During the same period, cigar smoking had become so popular among gentlemen in Britain and France that European trains introduced smoking cars to accommodate them, and hotels and clubs boasted smoking rooms. The after-dinner cigar, accompanied by glasses of port or brandy, also became a tradition. This ritual was given an added boost by the fact that the Prince of Wales, the future Edward VII and a leader of fashion, was a devotee, much to the annoyance of his mother, Queen Victoria, who disliked smoking.

Quote from "The History of Cigars," at www.cigars-review.org/history

Lady Evangeline, like Queen Victoria, disliked smoking. Unfortunately her husband, Lord Waverly, had been introduced to the custom of an after-dinner cigar while he was attending the sittings of the House of Lords in the year 1886. That year the debate over the Home Rule Bill for Ireland had been strenuous work, and shared discussion and relaxation with his fellow Peers over a glass of vintage port and a fine cigar after a hard day of political debate had been important. So, upon returning to the family seat, he had brought home with him his new habit—and a fine collection of cigars.

"I will not have that filthy habit in this house, Dorley," Lady Evangeline had said to her husband on the very first evening of his return, when, after dinner, Lord Waverly had settled back in his favorite chair and lit up. "The furnishings and I simply won't tolerate it," she added, gliding elegantly over and removing the cigar from his mouth, and then just as gracefully tossing it onto the fire, which burned merrily in the grate of the small retiring room they used in the evenings.

"But, bu . . .bu. . . ," Dorley stammered. "But the Prince of Wales—Bertie—smokes several a day, my dear. In the club it's a ritual; a gentlemen just has to smoke at least one cigar a day to be seen as worth knowing nowadays."

"If you must smoke, Dorley, well then, you must find some place to pursue this habit so that the . . . smoke does not pollute the house."

Because Lady Evangeline was a woman of strong will and a sharp tongue, Dorley replied, "Yes, Dear. As it's a pleasant evening, I think I'll take a walk about the grounds then." And he pulled himself up out of his comfortable chair, took a fresh cigar from the box and some vespas, and removed himself into the gardens.

Fortunately for Dorley, it was late summer at the time and the walk was most agreeable. But unfortunately, within a few weeks, the weather was turning cool, and by the time he was ready to indulge his after-dinner habit, it was becoming a bit too cold and dark to be roaming the grounds. Lord Waverly pondered this briefly before turning his steps to the fine stable building that stood behind the main house, and where quite a few fine horses were kept in great comfort.

He quickly discovered that the stable was the warmest place he could go to smoke, so he took to taking his nightly cigar there and inspecting the fine thoroughbreds he kept while he savored the smoke of his equally fine cigar.

The stable boys had a small cast iron stove that heated one end of the stable and that they sat about in their breaks. And as it got colder, his lordship often spent some time sitting by it, always alone, as was proper, and enjoying the gentle snuffling and blowing of the horse, the smell of healthy horseflesh, and the warmth, as he puffed on his cigar.

It was on such a night, but one when he had wandered into the stable later than usual, and unobserved, when he discovered Lionel's secret. It was actually no secret to many in Dorley's household and even Lady Evangeline had heard the maids discussing it. But Lord Waverly was a man of little experience, or interest, in sexual matters, having seen immeasurably more nakedness in the British museum's collection of Greek marbles than he ever had in real life. Even Lady Evangeline's body remained largely a mystery to him. It was common knowledge that his lordship was generally more concerned with matters of fashion and style and business than with estate gossip. Lady Evangeline also disapproved of gossip and may have heard about Lionel but would never have mentioned such a matter to her husband.

But on this night as Dorley sat puffing, leaning back in a comfortable chair that had appeared by the small stove on his second visit there, he heard voices and rustling in one of the further stalls and went to investigate—more from having nothing else to do than any great curiosity.

And then he discovered it. One of the stable boys was standing behind a young woman bending over with her skirts pulled up about her head and her drawers at her ankles, revealing her plump pink bottom and legs. And gliding in and out of her was Lionel's secret. Not that Dorley at that time knew it was Lionel's, though he assumed he was one of his stable boys. Lord Waverly gaped at what the young man had, his cigar forgotten and burning to ash as he watched Lionel's huge dick pumping the young woman.

The young woman's moans increased in frequency and pitch and became high squeals, and then she let out a big sigh. Lionel's hips beat faster against her backside until he pulled out, and Dorley's jaw dropped even lower as he saw Lionel in his full glory and the stable lad shot his seed in a long trail across the young woman's bottom and up to the roof.

Yes, Lionel had a whopper. Even if Lord Waverly had heard the rumors his wife, Lady Evangeline, had heard, he would still have been amazed.

The young woman pushed down her skirts and turned and Lionel squeezed a breast as they kissed long and deeply. Then the young woman pulled up her drawers and retied them while Lionel pulled up his woolen trousers and rebuttoned the fly and slipped his braces over his shoulders. Lionel straightened her maid's cap for her and she asked him, "When can we meet again?"

Dorley suddenly remembered the burning cigar in his hand and tiptoed guiltily back to the small stove and sat down as if he had been there all the time. But his mind wasn't with it. Even the fine cigar couldn't distract him from the memory of what he had just seen, and he had to unbutton his own fly and reach in—after checking to see no one was watching—and pull out his own engorging dick and fist it to completion.

That night he entered Lady Evangeline's bed and gave her a merry humping, such as he hadn't done for months, if not years.

The next night Dorley was nervous as he left the house and headed for the stables. There was a part of him that wanted to see what Lionel had and what he did with it again, and a part that strongly disapproved. He had spoken to his head groom, Mr. Peterson, casually about the stable staff, and after listening to Peterson tell him what trouble he was having deciding who to promote to be his assistant groom, since the previous one had just died of typhoid fever, Dorley discovered there were six stable lads and now had a list of names on a piece of paper in his pocket. He had even spent part of the day trying to surreptitiously determine which stable boy he had watched the previous night. But without success.

Now he approached his stables full of nervous excitement and was more interested in listening for voices and rustlings noises the horses didn't make, than in savoring his fine hand-rolled Cuban cigar. He was smoking one of five that had arrived just that day from the Duke of Westerbrook. They had been sent him as a gift, along with a note announcing that Westerbrook would like the pleasure of visiting Lord Waverly shortly. Dorley had sent an immediate invitation and was intrigued as to what had prompted the famous man's urge to visit him, as Westerbrook was one of the most fashionable men in London, a familiar of the Prince of Wales, and a great patron of the arts.

All in all Dorley had far too many things on his mind and sat on long after his cigar had burnt to ash and the butt end had been consigned to the small cast iron stove he sat near. But nothing happened that night.

The next night it happened again; he heard murmurs and rustlings not made by any horse, and he cautiously approached the noises. The sound of human voices moaning made him tremble. They were in a more distant stall this time, and it took Dorley some time to locate them in the shadows of the stable, away from the lamp hanging by the stove. In the dim light Dorley at first thought he was watching a rerun of the previous nights copulating, the huge penis of the stable body seemingly pumping in and out from between the pale round cheeks of a young woman's firm bottom. But when they were done and Lionel's seed had been spouted across the bent-over body before him and his partner stood up, Dorley felt himself blush from head to toe. Because it was only then, when they stood up and began pulling their trousers up that he realized he had been watching two young men at it. They both buttoned up their heavy workman's trousers and slipped their braces back over their shoulders, then kissed, and Lionel's companion asked "When can we meet again?"

Dorley gulped at hearing the question and fled back to the safety of his comfortable chair and the warm stove. But as had happened the previous time he had watched Lionel, he had to release his throbbing pole and gain release from the pressure built up inside him.

Dorley had been an only son and kept at home all his life, where he had been raised by a nanny and taught by two firm, but fair tutors. He knew he was not particularly intelligent and had led a sheltered youth. He had rarely seen another man's penis flaccid, and before seeing Lionel's monster had never seen one fully erect. And now that he had seen that one of his stable boys had an erection such as he had never imagined could exist, Dorley's mind was in a whirl. That night he again gave his wife, Lady Evangeline, a vigorous humping, and she responded unusually vocally.

The next day he discovered that the stable boy with the mammoth dick was named Lionel. But after two more evening visits to the barn, Dorley had seen no more of Lionel and his fucking activities.

Then Lord Westerbrook arrived, and there was a large dinner for all the ladies and gentlemen of the neighborhood. But so that Lady Evangeline wouldn't be forced to tolerate smoking in her house, Dorley took his honored guest and the other smoking gentlemen out to the stables. There they inspected the fine thoroughbreds Dorley kept before sitting about the small stove on folding chairs set up there for the occasion while puffing on their cigars, drinking brandy and port brought across from the house, and discussing business and politics. Dorley beamed happily as Lord Westerbrook told him he had been impressed by the horseflesh and nodded approvingly.

The following afternoon Lord Westerbrook took himself off for an after-lunch cigar. Dorley considered joining him, but Lady Evangeline gave him such a look of disapproval that he made an excuse. Lord Westerbrook's generous assurance he was happy to take a stroll alone for an hour or two to walk off the delightful lunch and enjoy his smoke was a great relief to Dorley. Lord Waverly instead went to visit his estate manger and discuss the repair of some tenant's cottages damaged in a recent storm.

The next day Lady Evangeline was called away to visit her sister who had suddenly taken ill. Consequently, the two gentlemen were left to their own devices.

Westerbrook hurried out immediately after lunch, "Time to go to the stables to enjoy my cigar, old man. What, ho," he shot at Dorley.

After dithering for a few minutes, Dorley decided to join him and took a cigar from the box and headed to the stables. But when he arrived at the stove, there was no one in sight, so he left his unlit cigar on the barrel that served the stable lads as a table, and wandered between the stalls and patted the noses of the horses he knew. Near the end of the row, though, he stopped; he had heard noises, but more—he could see two figures, and he scuttled back a few steps into the shadows. But he didn't leave; instead, he stood there mesmerized.

Inside the far stall he saw a man and, with a shock, he realized that it was Westerbrook. Yes, his lordship was standing naked, a pale thin body with a heavy coating of dark hair running up his torso, and he was removing Lionel's trousers in a very odd way. Westerbrook's hand had been at the buttons but then he was on his knees before the stable lad, slowly unbuttoning his fly still, but also nuzzling it as Lionel stood staring down at him and played a hand gingerly in his lordship's hair.

Once enough buttons had been parted, Westerbrook nuzzled his face deeper into the fly of Lionel's trousers and the stable boy swayed slightly and moaned. Then his lordship was reaching in and pulling Lionel's half-hard sausage free. Dorley almost couldn't believe his eyes.

"God, I thought it was a monster yesterday. How big will it get today, boy?" Westerbrook asked as he held the stable boy's huge penis in his hand, gripping it and bringing his mouth down to it.

He kissed the end of it. Then it was his pink tongue snaking out to lick the head of Lionel's cock and slobber all around it and slide up and down the firm, thick shaft. Lionel was obviously affected, as he now ran both hands roughly through his lordship's hair and was moving his hips in a back and forth motion and panting. Even from where he was, Dorley could see and hear that he was panting, and also see that the sausage had grown to its full size under the attentions of his lordship.

And Dorley could see the shine of the saliva that Westerbrook left coating the stable lad's cock as he licked it. Dorley stood dumbstruck as he watched what followed.

Westerbrook now opened his mouth, and the sausage disappeared into it slowly at first and moved in and out as he still gripped its root. But it finally disappeared completely. How he didn't choke on such a thing was a miracle, Dorley might have thought, if he was capable of thought just then. Instead, he watched as Westerbrook began to deep throat that massive tool. Bobbing his head up and down on it as Lionel's fingers tangled in his hair.

But suddenly Lord Westerbrook pulled off Lionel's piece and looked at what he was swallowing. "My god, even bigger than yesterday. Even bigger than old randy Randall told me it was," he exclaimed, before opening his mouth and again sucking the huge thing in until there was only the root left outside his lordship's mouth.

Dorley was more than stunned by all this; he was past any emotion now as he pulled his own throbbing tool from his own unbuttoned fly and jerked his fist up and down it rapidly, with his other hand pressed over his mouth so he didn't make any sounds. He came in an explosion of cum that seemed to pulse out endlessly across the cobbled floor of the stable.

Inside the stall Westerbrook had given up his lollipop and stood up, and was now lying himself back on some hay bales and lifting and parting his legs.

"Do me this way today," he ordered in a commanding voice.

The stable boy rapidly shed his trousers, saying, "Whatever you want, my Lord," politely but rather mumbling it as he walked in between Lord Westerbrook's spread thighs and probed the hole before him with saliva soaked fingers while his other hand went to fisting his lordship rather slowly. What His Lordship had was far from small itself, Dorley observed at this time.

Then it was the flared purple head of his cock that Lionel was positioning at Westerbrook's hair-rimmed asshole. Once he'd slowly dragged the head around Westerbrook's puckered rim, and again, then . . . he punched it in. Dorley almost fainted as Lord Westerbrook arched and jerked and cried, "Yeow," but then His Lordship was yelling, "Harder boy. Harder. Faster."

Lionel did as he was bid and pounded his hefty meat long and hard in and out of Lord Westerbrook's rear entry. So long and hard that Dorley actually felt himself harden up again and had to stroke off again, spilling a dribble of seed onto the cold stoned floor.

The finale in the stall came soon after. Lionel slamming his hips against his Lordship's ass, while fisting Westerbrook's cock. The peer grasped at his own nipples and shouted, "Ride me. Ride me. Fuck, I'm coming," and spouted his cream all up his belly and over his chest. At the same time, Dorley witnessed the familiar stiffening and sudden shuddering jerks that signaled Lionel's own release.

Lionel pulled free soon after, but Westerbrook wasn't done. "Lick it up boy, all of it," the Lord ordered, and when Lionel looked confused he ordered him roughly, "Get on your knees boy. Lick your cum up as it oozes out of my arse, boy."

Lionel hesitated, and Westerbrook aimed a kick at his balls and repeated his instructions adding, "I've told you already that I'll ruin you if you don't satisfy me."

Lord Waverly was shocked. He was outraged in fact that a guest in his house should treat one of his staff in such a way. Lionel hurried to comply and vigorously licked between the thighs and butt cheeks of his Lordship until there was nothing left to lick up. And Dorley watched, fascinated, both aroused by the sight but repelled by Westerbrook's incivility.

As they dressed afterwards, Dorley heard Lord Westerbrook making Lionel an offer he was unlikely to refuse. "What are you paid here?" he asked Lionel.

"Five pounds a year, my Lord, " the stable boy replied hurrying to get his boots on.

"You'll come and be my stable boy," Westerbrook said and laughed loudly, "I'll give you twenty pounds a year. I'll speak to the head groom right away and arrange it," he added, and Dorley, who had finally regained some of his senses, hurried away before he was discovered.

Dorley could hardly look at Westerbrook when that gentleman reappeared in the drawing room for afternoon tea, looking as immaculate and superior as ever. And after dinner the two gentlemen retired to the stable for a cigar as usual but smoked in near silence before returning to the house and immediately retiring.

The next day Westerbrook went out early and returned bad tempered, he went out for an after-lunch cigar but was back in under half an hour, and that night at dinner he announced he was leaving for London the following morning. Lady Evangeline, who had returned that morning, tried politely to convince him to stay, but Dorley was pleased to see she didn't try too hard. So the following day they stood side by side on the gravel drive at the bottom of the steps leading up to the main entrance of the house and waved Lord Westerbrook good-bye as his carriage rolled off along the driveway.

"I can't say I was taken with your friend Lord Westerbrook," Lady Evangeline said casually as they returned to the house, and her husband surprised her by grunting as if he agreed with her.

After dinner that night, Dorley took a cigar from the box as usual and retired to the stables to smoke it, but he had barely lit up and started to puff when there was a shuffling sound and his stable boy, Lionel, stood before him, cap in hand and wearing his good clean Sunday clothes.

"Beg pardon your lordship, but may I speak?"

"Um, . . . uh, of course. Of course," Dorley stuttered in surprise, hardly able to look at the young man.

"Mr. Peterson the head groom spoke to me yesterday, sir, and I am most grateful to you for your generosity. I'm to be his assistant now he says, and on seven pounds a year, which is a right fine sum. And my wife and I shall have our own cottage." He hesitated then, and turned his cap nervously in his hands. "Not that I was going to accept the offer Lord Westerbrook made me, sir. Umm, I have a wife too. And I have heard he is not an easy master, if you will forgive me for saying so, sir. And he doesn't have the fine stable of horses as is here, your lordship."

"Well, yes, um, Mr. Peterson is pleased with your work Lionel. He was keen to keep you," Dorley reassured him nervously.

"Thank you, sir," Lionel replied.

"Good. All settled then," Dorley said loudly, uncomfortable at having such a personal conversation with his stable boy and feeling his own cock twitch as he was unable not to imagine Lionel with his huge dick erect, and spilling its seed.

Lionel dipped his head respectfully and sniffed. Quite obviously, he sniffed. "Them cigars all smells different, don't they, your lordship?" he added, "But it's not a bad smell."

Dorley looked up and frowned as he thought about this, "Oh, you've smelt them before then?" he replied, twisting the one in his hand about.

"Yes sir. The smell is mighty strong close by," Lionel replied, "I'll be off then, sir," he added, bobbing his head respectfully and replacing his cap on his head as he left.

Dorley puffed away as he considered what had been said. And when his cigar was finished he threw the butt into the cast-iron stove and returned to his house, and to his wife, Lady Evangeline, in their small retiring room.

"You look unusually pleased with yourself," she remarked when he joined her.

"Oh? Do I, dear?"

"Yes, you do. And when are you going to give up that dirty smoking habit?" she asked.

"Give up? Oh, not for a long time yet, dear, I enjoy my cigars far too much to give them up," he answered her.

Suits

by habu

It was a steamy, smoke-filled night at Hernando's, and I and
the other two guys had been dancing to the music on the small stage
for twenty minutes. I was already down to the ten-gallon hat, the pinto
pony vest, the cowboy boots, and the low-slung belt and six-gun
holsters with the even lower slung eight-inch gun swinging in between
and nothing else on when I felt the hand on the ankle of one of my
boots.

The dude clinging to my boot looked cooler than a cucumber
despite the heat and the indoor smog and even though he was wearing
a suit—a finely tailored Brooks Brothers navy blue pinstripe silk suit
that was cut close to his well-cut body. He looked like money all over.
His pale blue dress shirt was as finely and closely cut to the perfect
curves and bulges of his body as his suit was, and the gold studs in his
shirt cuffs and his Rolex watch sparkled in beams from the strobing
lights overhead. He was flashing a set of ultrawhite, perfectly capped
teeth at me in a full-lipped, sensuous mouth. His teeth were clinching a
fat cigar. He also was flashing a fifty-dollar bill in his well-manicured
hand.

Having gotten my attention by grabbing my boot as I was
undulating on the stage above him, stroking myself off, not far from

giving the crowd the thrill it had come to see, he twirled the cigar in his mouth and sucked on it suggestively for a moment to center my attention and then yelled up to me through the loud music and the din of cat calls and stale suggestions. "You fuck me? More of this if it's good for me."

Fifty dollars? His tie alone was worth four times that. Gawd, it looked like the cigar he was sucking was worth that much. An insult. I was having offers twice that high thrown at me by the plumbers and electricians sitting all around him. I crouched down and shot my load across the nice lapels of his $800 Brooks Brothers suit, and then I went home that night and fucked my bass-voiced boyfriend until he warbled soprano. And I did it for free.

Three nights later I was at my other evening job, the more humbling one, as a car hop at the Honeywell Hotel. They made me wear a monkey suit there; I much prefer my cowboy outfit at Hernando's. It had been air conditioned and I was watched when I wore that one. I liked being watched; I was built to be watched. Here at Honeywells I was invisible; just part of the service in getting into and out of the hotel in a jiff. But at least here I got to jockey Porsche Boxsters—at least as far as the parking lot over in the shadows beside and behind the hotel.

I was contemplating being invisible when a honey of a silver Maserati Quattoporte drove up to the entrance and out stepped . . . the suit from Hernando's. At least he was still noticing me—and he was still sucking on a cigar. He picked up on who I was right off, and I was afraid he might take a swing at me for messing up his Brooks Brothers—but he didn't.

He was all flashy smiles and knowing looks. And he had been slumming the other night. Tonight he was wearing a lustrous brown Armani suit, easily worth three times what the blue pinstripe the other night had been worth, and he had on an ochre silk shirt under that, a flashy silk tie, and diamond cufflinks. This time the cigar was a long, thin panatela. The Armani was just as expensively and closely cut as the suit of the other night was. The man was dripping money. It was almost like I could walk along behind him and pick up gold coins as he shot them out of his ass like a bunny with diarrhea.

Two hours later he reappeared through the hotel entrance. Another one of the car hops reached for his ticket, but he held off from giving it to that guy and looked around until he spotted me. He walked over, flashing that big "see what I've got and you don't" smile at me and handed me the ticket. But he also had $200 in folded fifties in the hand holding the ticket, and he wouldn't let loose of either of those or my hand as he said in a husky whisper, "Shall we up the ante?"

I was going off duty then anyway. And two hundred bucks meant a lot to me—obviously far more than it meant to him. When I drove the Maserati around, I didn't get out of the driver's seat; I just leaned over and flipped open the passenger seat door. This was a signal to him, a gauntlet, so to speak. If we were going to do this thing, I was going to do the driving. I liked the idea of the $200, but if he thought he was going to get off as cheaply as that, he was mistaken. Tonight was going to cost him a whole hell lot more than $200.

He got in the passenger side without hesitation. I took the panatela he was sucking out of his mouth and stuck it in mine—just to show him who was in control. He gave it up with a slight, knowing smile. Then I fisted the stick shift and he fisted my stick as I drove him into the parking lot and back to the corner where I had my Chevy van parked. I clicked open the sliding side door to the van, and the suit got in without hesitation and whistled in appreciation. I had it outfitted for love. Smoked windows; floor, sides, and ceiling covered in padded sapphire blue velour; straps anchored strategically here and there; and an easily accessible sound system with speakers embedded all around. And that stool. He'd be introduced to the stool later.

I told him to take off his shoes in my home—just like they do in the Orient. And while he docilely did that, I climbed into the van, stripped off the hated car jockey's uniform, clicked the side door shut, and turned on the sound system. I set the cigar in an ashtray embedded in the wall panel and selected Lebanese music with a good strong beat and a tortured-voice singer singing in a manner that would disguise most any yowling coming from inside the van. I planned on there being some yowling.

First thing I did was tie up the dude's right wrist to a strap in the ceiling of the van, a little behind the front seat. I didn't want him going anywhere or getting the notion he was going to be in charge. He hunched there, in his Armani suit, his free hand searching between my thighs.

I stripped the Rolex from his left wrist and, after entertaining him with how well balanced it was when I hung it on my hard cock and spun it around for him, I tossed it into one of his shoes. I didn't want the reminder of money ticking away while I worked here. Then I got his fist off my cock, where he had found a mushroom cap silver stud that flashed in the overhead bulb just as brightly as his diamond cufflinks did, and strapped his left wrist up to the ceiling.

I unbelted and unzipped him, and peeled the Armani trousers and Calvin Klein briefs off his legs. And I wasn't delicate about it. I heard a rip and so did he, but neither one of us showed that we cared. I was moving with determination and he was already wide-eyed and giving little panting sounds and murmured moanings. He had seen my eight inches in full erection already. He knew what I was packing for him.

He was crouched there on his knees now, panting, in fine silk socks held up with braces under his knees and above his well-muscled calves, but still fully decked out in suit coat, shirt, and tie. I crouched between his spread knees, letting my cock snake up under the tail of his shirt and bedevil his navel while our lips were heavily engaged in a sloppy kiss. I unbuttoned the two middle buttons of his shirt, just enough so that I could spread the expensive, rustling silk and expose a puffed up nipple. Then I lowered my head and pushed his tie aside with my chin and worked his nipple through the opening of his shirt with my tongue and teeth.

He was moaning for me. Begging to be fucked.

I raised his legs, one at a time, and tied them to straps in the ceiling toward the back of the van. He was trussed up now and hanging like a deer over a campfire, face up to the ceiling. I threw a leg over his belly and put my hands on the back of the front seat on either side of his head and clicked my silver cock stud against his white teeth until he opened for me and gave me head. He gave me good head, moaning and groaning all of the time at the length and width and hardness of me. This is what he was paying for. This is what he was going to get.

When I was bored with this, I pulled my cock out of his mouth and threw my leg back over him. He watched in eye-silted lust and interest as I opened a side glove compartment and took out a handful of condom packets. I opened a packet and rolled a condom onto my cock. Then I extracted a leather-studded cock ring and wrapped that around the base of my cock. The last item I pulled out of the compartment was a small bottle of KY. All the time he was whimpering for me, begging for me to get inside him.

I reached over for the cigar. He showed great interest as he followed the arc of that from ashtray to between his legs, and he arched his back and groaned a bit as I played around his rim and just inside his hole with the panatela, teasing his puckering hole. He bore his ass down on the cigar and tried to draw it inside him, but I just laughed and returned it to the ashtray.

He did look a little concerned then when I reached up and undid the cuffs on his shirt on both sides and extracted his diamond cufflinks and then tied them with string to my cock ring. I was chuckling about him getting his money's worth out of this fuck. But he didn't seem all that amused.

He probably thought I was going to take my time and open him up real well for the fuck. But he was wrong there. I soaked down my cock with the KY and squirted enough into his hole for it to be beneficial for me. But then I was rimming him with my bulbous mushroom cap and pressuring his hole and making little forced entries and pulling back a little and then worrying the tight, unready hole again. And then, when I'd gotten the cap all the way in, I just thrust in and bottomed with one lunge. And he yowled to the velour ceiling, hitting a high A even stronger and truer than the Lebanese musician was doing on the background music. And he continued to yowl, first in pain and then in consuming desire, as I picked up the beat of the music and fucked him and fucked and fucked him.

As I fucked him, I bunched up that silk ochre-colored shirt of his in my fists and literally ripped it off his body, pulling the shreds of it from underneath his tie and the brown Armani suit coat. The dude didn't seem to care; he was swinging his body against my plunging cock with the beat of the music and warbling right along with the Lebanese singer. He came in great spoutings long before I did.

Sometime during the fucking, I felt the diamond cufflinks come loose and work themselves up the dude's passage with the thrustings of my cock. The dude gave little yipping sounds at this added fiber to his ass's diet, but he made no objection. He wasn't objecting to anything now except to the possibility that I might stop stroking his ass. I almost went on a laughing jag mid fuck at the image of how he'd be shitting diamonds for the next day or so. Thinking about that being close to the meaning of being filthy rich.

When I was spent, I leaned into him and encircled his torso with my arms and felt the fast beating of his heart next to mine through the shredded ochre silk until he had calmed down and I had started to reload. He was sighing and whispering endearments to me, telling me how good I was and hoping I wasn't finished taking him.

I wasn't finished. Not by a long shot. This wasn't nearly expensive enough of a fuck for this dude yet.

I released both his legs and arms, but I immediately turned him and reattached his wrists to straps at the base of the front seat on either side. He didn't object. He was licking his lips. I was giving him exactly what he was seeking from me. I pulled over a low, velour-covered stool with a hole in the seat and forced the dude down on top of it on his lower belly. His cock and balls were poked through the hole and he found that he was encased in a sleeve around his cock and sacks around his balls, which were the business end of a cock milking machine. I strapped his hips to the stool so he couldn't extract his cock and then turned on the machine. The machine started to slowly contract the sleeve around his cock and undulate over it, teasing his cock to engorge and discharge. And the sacks around his balls also contracted and squeezed in a fascinating rhythm. He seemed to like this, and began moaning almost immediately. He'd maybe have second thoughts after he'd shot off the first time and found the machine wasn't satisfied with that.

I crouched up where he could see me and changed the spent condom for a fresh one and lathered it down with KY. And then I was behind him, making him push his knees wide, his butt waving in the air. I straddled him, my thighs on either side of his waist, above his stretched thighs, my hands on his shoulder blades. And then I reared my hips back and thrust my sheathed cock inside him and pumped hard and fast.

He was singing a loud duet again with the Lebanese singer to the heavy beat of the music.

I tore the coat off his back while I was fucking him and the stool was milking him, and I put it in front of his face and tore the lining out. He didn't care. He was going over the moon with what I and the stool were doing to him. I pulled the expensive silk necktie around his neck to his back and used it as reins as I did a bull bucking rodeo exhibit on his buttocks. I could feel the diamond cufflinks churning around inside him and he could too. I could tell that by the screams of passion he was making. The Lebanese singer was reaching a climax in his yowling and so were the dude and I. The dude shuddered and came, and then moaned as he discovered that the stool wasn't finished with him. And then I gave a cowboy whoop and came as well.

After a second and then a third ride, and continuous attention from the stool, I was finished with him. I turned off the stool and untied him, and he just huddled there in thank-you whimpers. As a parting gesture, I untied his necktie, rolled the spent condom off my dick, and wiped my dick and then his asshole with the silk tie and dropped the whole wad beside him on the van floor. Then I reached over to the ashtray for the cigar and stuffed it in his mouth. His gaze told me that he was still in love. It didn't seem like anything I was going to do was going to tell this guy where he could stuff all his money, as far as I was concerned. Still, I figured when the semen had drained out of his eyes, he'd come to his senses and survey the damage I had done to all his expensive stuff and get a little mad.

I put my car jockey duds back on and made sure he could see where I was leaving the keys to his Maserati. And then I left him there, in the back of my Chevy van, and walked back over to the entrance of the hotel. Within minutes a studly black guy gave me a ticket and a look, and, when I'd driven around his shiny black Mercedes CLS55 AMG, we were driving off to his up-town penthouse apartment, where I fucked him silly and he fed me breakfast, begged for and received my bone a second time, and then brought me back to the hotel for my now-deserted Chevy van.

Two days later, I was dancing on the stage of Hernando's when I felt a fist wrap around the ankle of my boot. There, gazing up at me with love-struck eyes, another cigar swirling between his teeth, was the suit, now outfitted in a black sharkskin $3,000-plus Valentino, diamond cufflinks cleaned and polished and gleaming in beams from the overhead strobe lights—holding a wad of hundred-dollar bills in his other fist.

Wanting me again.

Cigars in the Stable

by Sabb

"Getting caught up in Riddleman's murder was frightening," I blurted out over coffee.

"Wasn't that some sort of sex crime?" Amanda asked, leaning forward excitedly.

The ohs, and ahs went around the table, and I wished I hadn't said anything, because everyone was looking at me—and expecting more.

Over dessert the conversation had turned to murder, which wasn't surprising, because Kirk Glendenning, the famous murder mystery writer, was staying with our hosts, the Luckmans.

The truth was that for a while I had been more than frightened. And in answer to Amanda's question, well, I knew there had been a lot of sex just before the murder, but as to why it was committed, I had an idea that it had more to do with tobacco and cigarettes.

"If I hadn't been somebody in this town, and had a good lawyer available right away, I am sure the police would have tried hard to pin it on me at the beginning," I said seriously, remembering when I had realized how serious my situation might be and had gotten scared.

"Why was that?" Kirk asked. "Why was it so frightening?"

"Because I had no alibi. They found me in the barn asleep with a big hangover, and there was a dead body in the house. Now what does a crime writer do about setting up an alibi that is watertight?" I asked, wanting the conversation to move on.

"We all know you were there that night," Maria said though. "Larry and I saw you. You were the singer. But why on earth did the police think you might have been involved?"

There was silence in the room, and someone coughed. I think it was me.

"No real reason, I was just there and at first they didn't know who I was. They thought I was a nobody or . . . um. And Riddleman was a very rich and powerful man. And they knew that his guests that night were also all rich and well known around here, so they didn't want to have to start questioning them and causing themselves aggravation."

Randall Luckman changed the subject then, and I helped him. But later after dinner Kirk Glendenning cornered me and asked me into the Luckmans' study.

"Do you mind my asking you, what really happened that night? As far as you know of, of course? And just how you were caught up in it?" Kirk was asking me these questions politely, and I wondered if the creative wheels were turning under the crop of silver-streaked curls he sported.

"I was singing that night at the function," I replied, knowing most of the people at the dinner table knew something of what had happened already and could tell him. "And afterwards I did some partying and then fell asleep in the stables behind the house. I woke up to find two policemen looking down at me."

What I didn't say was that I had been naked and hung over, with the cum of the dead man and his mysterious companion filling my stomach, when they had found me. I had given a fairly accurate outline of the night's main events to the police in the interview room at the Newcastle police station. But I had never told anyone the more interesting details of the sex I'd had that night.

But for some reason I told a lot more to Kirk Glendenning that night, than I had told anyone previously.

"I was into my second-to-last number when I saw them. Riddleman was a big man, and he was over by one of the French doors that let onto the terrace. He was moving a thick cigar about in his mouth suggestively, and I was having trouble keeping my eyes off him," I told him, remembering more about that night than I had for years.

"I've never smoked, but cigars had always fascinated me. Our host was big and powerful, with a reputation for rough sex, and was useful to know. I also hadn't missed the dark Latin looker standing by the next set of open doors fucking his good Cuban cigar slowly in and out between his lips as his eyes held mine."

Unfortunately, those eyes had me getting hard, and my dick was straining against my well-fitted black evening pants. I was getting uncomfortable standing there in front of the crowd, trying to maintain my composure and finish my last song for the night. I couldn't even attempt to ease the pressure or cover my growing erection in the position I was in, standing next to the grand piano in front of a crowd of two hundred of the best citizens Merewether Heights had to offer.

I have an excellent tenor voice. But I had decided in my mid twenties that I would never make it big as a singer. I knew that

74

decision resulted more from my distaste for the constant struggle unknowns have in proving themselves and the experience of two years spent living in hotels and short-term holiday flats with neurotic young sopranos, than to any failings in my own talent.

In short, I liked the comfortable easy life and had finally taken up the opportunity to enter the family business at a senior level. But the desire to sing was still strong, and though it was eight years since I'd given up the professional dream, at the time of Riddleman's murder I was still performing regularly. I sang voluntarily with two choirs, and occasionally I sang at private functions. I still do. And I've always demanded a very sizeable donation to my favorite charity from anyone wanting me to perform just for them, which ensured I wasn't called on to do every wedding in town. But I was still kept busy.

That night's performance had been requested some months before, and I had been surprised, as I had never met Riddleman personally and would have expected some shapely female in something low cut to be more to the taste of the older Merewether Heights crowd there. But then again the evening's host, Oscar Riddleman, was a slightly mysterious man, with unusual tastes, who apparently liked to have anything he took a fancy to. And I have been told that back then I was still much to be fancied.

I hit the high note at the end of my last song of the evening, and, closing my eyes, managed to hold it long enough to impress the crowd. They clapped me a bit more enthusiastically than politeness required, which gave me a lift that added to the sexual heat I was already feeling.

Riddleman was heavy set and looked to be in his early fifties, more muscle than fat, I thought, with a full head of grizzled dark hair and sharp dark eyes. While I was politely taking the applause, he sucked on his cigar and turned it around between his full lips. He moved it from side to side in his mouth as he smiled at me and looked me up and down. He had stripped me naked with that look, and I wasn't really keen on him, but occasionally I liked that sort of powerful domination.

But then my eyes were drawn back over to the Latin. He was the perfect Latin playboy type—lean, tall, and dark haired, with dark smoldering eyes and a seductive smile. And removing his cigar from his mouth, he give me a big smile just then and shook his free hand as if he had burnt his fingers. I smiled back. He was telling me I was hot. And his eyes traveled down my body and stopped at my crotch and the smile got bigger. I knew I was showing, and I just smiled back. I knew he'd like what I had down there.

Phew. I was mesmerized by the cigar play and didn't know which one to look at. Then Riddleman jerked his head, indicating the door beside him, and turned and walked outside. I looked over to the Latin as I left my place beside the piano and saw that he was also slipping outside on to the terrace. I pushed through the crowd to follow him.

Outside the semicircular raised terrace was lit by hundreds of colorful candle-filled paper lanterns, and in their gentle moody light, I found the Latin leaning on the balustrade at the top of the wide staircase that swept down to the rose garden. He smiled and pulled a big, thick, hand-rolled Cuban cigar from his inside picket as his eyes locked on mine. The big cigar was rolled delicately between his fingers. He sniffed it slowly before it was gently wrapped in his full lips, where he twisted it about, wetting it, and moved it in and out before he lit it.

Then he was sucking it to a bright glow before a thin wisp of smoke rose up from the tip, as he removed it from between his lips and exhaled.

"A fine performance," he said, with a big grin.

I smiled back at him, "I aim to please," I said.

"Riddleman likes to be pleased," he replied, and he laughed, but then he was heading down the staircase. I followed him.

Our host was nowhere in sight. The tip of the Latin's cigar danced in and out of my sight as we left the rose-lined path and crossed the lawn beyond. Then the cigar tip disappeared, and a moment later I reached a gate in the hedge surrounding the garden and went through it.

"Several witnesses apparently remembered seeing us leave the terrace," I told Kirk. "I was amazed at what people at the party had noticed. And, fortunately, after I had told my side to the police, they had found plenty of them who'd support me in the parts that mattered."

Beyond the gate was a short shrub-lined path where the smell of gardenias hung heavy in the air. Then I was in a cobbled yard and a high-gabled building was before me and the cigar tip was wavering as a door opened, letting out a wash of light. I entered the stable building ahead of the Latin, and inside was my other cigar-loving admirer, Riddleman. But not looking like his guests remembered. He was now sitting on a tartan rug that was tossed over a pile of hay bales, and he was leaning back with his pants and shoes off and his legs spread wide, showing me something he had to be proud of.

I had no trouble knowing what he wanted me for, as he had a thick, hard cock in one hand while the other still held his cigar. It was a toss-up if his dick or his cigar was longest. But his tool was certainly thickest. And I wondered what he had in mind for later, excited by him now, but worried I might have trouble taking what he had on offer.

"About time," he growled in a possessive way, showing perfect teeth in a big lascivious smile.

If I had been getting hard before, I was even harder now, knowing I was in for a three-way adventure. I turned to see that the Latin playboy had come up behind me, and he pushed me back around so I was facing Riddleman. Then his hands were running over my chest and belly and down, and he was unzipping me, pushing my pants and briefs down and letting my engorged dick free at last. It showed them both just how interested I was in what was going on.

"I don't mind a bit of singing, but this is more my kind of entertainment. Aye, Luca?" Riddleman growled with his eyes fixed on my tool, which I was sure was a match for his own in length, if not in thickness.

I sighed and moaned in relief at standing free and then sighed again and reached back to pull Luca's mouth to mine, as his long fingers found my cock and he began to stroke me. But he still had that cigar in his other hand and the smoke was curling up and stinging my eyes occasionally as he ran the hand holding it around my body. Then he had his hand low and I felt something pressing at the slit in my cock head and I looked down to see the wet tapered end of his hand rolled cigar being pressed into the tiny opened slit and rotated. I whimpered at the sight, writhing and moaning now, trapped inside his arms with my pants around my ankles, dripping and ready to explode.

"Yes. Yes. Give his dick a taste of a real cigar," Riddleman was crooning, leaning forward for a better view, wide eyed and panting, and finally taking my cock in his fist.

Then the cigar was gone and I fell back against Luca, moaning and pulling his face to mine again and kissing him deeply as I shot my load straight at Riddleman, whose tight wet mouth descended on me and cleaned me up.

I stepped out of my pants as Luca pushed me forward to the hay bales next to Riddleman, and I knelt on the tartan rug and rested my chest on the rug-covered higher bales of hay, presenting my now twitching ass to the two of them.

Strong fingers pulled my cheeks apart, and I felt something thin working its way into me easily, sliding in and going deep, and I knew it was Riddleman's cigar. He pulled it back out, almost to the end, then fucked me with it, rotating it inside me and giving me a surprising thrill as the end moved across my prostrate and stretched and pulled my channel. Then he lifted it, stretching my hole, and something else entered me below it and I turned to see both men looking on with lustful fascination, stroking themselves as they worked their cigars in unison in and out of my ass.

I moaned because I loved what they were doing to me, and then I moaned louder, seeing Luca's elegant long cock for the first time. It looked almost cruel with its curved shaft and mushroom cap, and his dark knob was almost like the end of one if his cigars.

I rested my cheek against the tartan-covered hay as I looked back at them, and my hand reached under me and started playing with my own tool and tugging at my balls.

Luca left his cigar inside me, minding his place, as he stepped back and stripped off. I sighed at how good he looked and wanted him to get on and fuck me himself. But when he removed his cigar, Riddleman removed his also and bent to lick my rim and wet my entrance. It hardly needed it after the double cigar fuck I had been getting. But he obviously enjoyed it, and when he thought I was wet enough, he slipped on a condom and stepped between my legs. I jerked away with a gasp as he began to enter me roughly, and I let him know he was going too fast. And I was sure he liked being rough.

Luca knelt beside me and alternated stroking his fingers over my butt cheeks and flicking them stingingly with his fingertips as Riddleman worked his way in, stretching me painfully, as I whimpered loudly. But then Luca distracted me more by wrapping his hand around my dick and stroking it, while running his other hand over my back, pushing my shirt up and out of the way as he worked firm fingers over the muscles of my back. Finally he lifted my head and took my mouth in a kiss, stifling my cry, as Riddleman bottomed painfully and roughly inside me.

Luca worked his way under me and was soon sitting on the hay in front of me so I had his curved tool fucking my throat as Riddleman plowed my channel. My hips moved in rhythm with Riddleman's controlled fucking, and Luca's hands strayed and explored. He was pinching my nipples, massaging my back, and then took hold of my hair, working my mouth on him as he wanted, till he pumped his cream into me. Riddleman came at about the same time, and soon after his cock slurped out. I felt empty then—and annoyed that I hadn't had Luca's curved sword inside me. But I discovered he reloaded quickly, and in a few minutes Luca had moved in behind me and was feeding that long thin cock into me. And while holding a fresh cigar in one hand and a glass of champagne in the other, Riddleman sat down beside me and watched, leaning forward for a good view of Luca's cock working its magic in and out of my ass.

When Luca was done, we all drank champagne and rested, and he and Riddleman sucked on their cigars and watched as I stroked myself back to hardness.

Then Riddleman told me to stand up and, pulling me between his spread thighs, sucked my cock head in between his lips like he sucked his cigars in. He worked me until I was as big as I was going to get, and then I got to fuck the dark and mysterious Luca as Riddleman watched up close and his cigar played in my asshole.

The champagne flowed freely all night and so did the cum of the three of us, but I have an idea the other two drank a lot less than I did, I told Kirk. I didn't remember drinking more than three or four glasses but must have drunk a lot more, because at some point I woke up and found myself lying naked and alone on the rug covered hay in the now dimly lit barn. I'd tried to get up and find my clothes and leave, but the stable building spun around and I almost blacked out, so I fell back, deciding I was staying there till I'd slept it off.

I finally woke up with a throbbing head to find a uniformed policeman shaking me and a man in a badly fitting suit looking down at me. It had seemed like some kind of joke to start with. Embarrassing, as I was lying there naked in front of these strangers as well as hung over, but still a joke. And I had asked them what the hell they were doing there and could they get out and leave me alone.

Instead, they had ordered me up and looked at me like they knew just what I had been up to the previous night.

"So, why did you kill him?" the suited guy asked.

I shook my head and tried to sit up.

"What are you talking about?" I muttered in a slurred voice, confused.

"Your host. I reckon he didn't pay up. Was that why? He wasn't happy with the service?" the suit asked, smiling nastily. "An escort. Isn't that what guys like you are called?" he added as if it was a big joke

That was when I started to get angry—and frightened.

"Turned out Riddleman was found lying naked on his bed in the morning. Dead. With a bullet through his temple. The mysterious Luca had disappeared and they never found out who he really was or where he's gone," I said to Kirk Glendenning.

"Ah," said Kirk. "Sounds like you had a lucky escape."

"Yes I did. But only because a lot of people had seen Luca during the evening, and one of the caterers had actually seen him and Riddleman return to the house together at around 3:00 AM. The security firm had a man there. A car left the car park at 4:00 AM, and the driver was picked up on the security cameras. Otherwise—" I shrugged.

It had been a difficult time.

"So, what was it all about?" Kirk had muttered more to himself than me.

"About?" I said, "Why, cigarettes of course. They talked about them while we fucked. Riddleman had factories somewhere producing imitation Marlboro cigarettes as well as cigars. And I am sure that Luca was running the operation for him."

Kirk looked at me, "But Riddleman's estate was declared bankrupt wasn't it? I thought they couldn't trace any assets?"

"Yes. But he lived like a king. His house was owned by a Jersey Island registered corporation, and nothing else was in his name either, so they had no choice. The house was sold later for twenty million dollars and the money just disappeared into a Jersey bank."

We were silent for a few minutes; then Kirk turned to me. "I believe you have the world's greatest cigar collection," he said nervously, giving me a look I had seen on the faces of a lot of men, a look that told me I was still fancied.

"Yes. I do. Would you like me to show it to you?" I asked, smiling a smile at him that told him a whole lot more about what I wanted to show him.

Picky, Picky

by habu

The young man's hand was trembling as he handed the creamy vellum envelope embossed with the FGCC crest over to the older man. Edward Winslow held the younger man's finger between his and the underside of the envelope for an extra couple of seconds before taking the envelope and placing it carefully on the top of the cigarette table beside him. He puffed on his cigar and smiled a satisfied smile to himself. He wanted Bill Brewster to tremble at the thought of handing over that envelope. It was final nail in this particular coffin.

Bill Brewster shifted nervously in his crackled-leather-covered Chippendale lounge chair in the dim corner of the First Gentlemen's Covenant Club smoking room and moved his slender, finely manicured hands together in a tented position, his fingertips centering between his patrician-shaped nose and his full, dry lips. He was doing all he could do to control the trembling of his hands, and he didn't want Winslow to see the trepidation his face surely revealed. He wasn't looking directly at his boss at First Families Securities, but Edward Winslow was looking directly at him and was smiling, clearly enjoying not just the young man's resignation but also his discomfort.

A tall, fine-figured Hispanic young male in a smartly tailored black silk uniform materialized at the side of Winslow's chair and set down a snifter of port. In withdrawing his hand, the servant barely brushed Winslow's hand with his. The senior partner of First Families Securities, the son of a son of a son going back to the arrival of the Mayflower on America's shores—the very prize that qualified Winslow for membership in the Beacon Hill First Gentlemen's Covenant Club—twitched his hand back, almost as if he'd been shot, and sent the port in his glass into a brief tempest.

"Damn Mexicans," Winslow muttered, as the servant moved silently behind the two chairs and, appearing at Bill Brewster's elbow, quietly slid the second snifter of port on the cigarette table beside the younger man.

"The old club's going to the damn Mexicans," Winslow continued to mutter. "At least the darkies they had in here before knew to wear gloves."

Bill Brewster picked up the snifter and moved it toward his mouth. But his hand was trembling so hard that he had to take the crystal vessel in his other hand as well to hold it steady. He took a nervous gulp from the glass—quite out of character for a son of a son of a son, who had equal rights to FGCC membership to those Winslow had. But these were circumstances he'd never faced before.

It wasn't until this evening that Winslow had fully believed Brewster would actually go through with it. The room key in that vellum envelope lying beside Winslow's snifter settled that question.

Winslow snapped his fingers, and the liveried attendant appeared at his side.

"Casa Blanca Jeroboam. No, two. Now."

The servant vanished in search of the cigar humidor behind the massive mahogany long bar.

85

Winslow looked back over at Brewster, who was breathing heavily, obviously trying to contain himself. This had been a campaign of the older man's for nearly a year. When Winslow had offered the younger man the broker's position, he had made it clear the extent to which Brewster was to show his gratitude. Brewster was a natural for the firm and looked the part perfectly, but he had majored in partying and tennis at Harvard, where only his name had stood him in good stead from being tossed out on his tail, and he normally could not have expected to have been given a position in the firm, despite his lineage.

The attendant reappeared, and Winslow snatched one of the cigars from him and motioned with an irritation usually reserved for the slow of mind for the other one to be placed on top of the vellum envelope. He hissed his disapproval that the Mexican had handled the cigars; they should have been delivered on a white linen napkin.

"No training whatsoever," Winslow muttered. "Can't train a Mexican. Heh, William?"

"Ye . . . yes, Edward, that . . . that's right." Brewster was obviously uncomfortable, but it wasn't about Winslow's berating of the servant, because he added the unnecessary. "Training would be a waste. He'll be slipping back across the border as soon as he's made a few bucks."

"Next time on a napkin, Jose," Winslow hissed.

"Yes, sir," the servant said, his eyes downcast, as he backed into the shadows.

"You know his name?" Brewster asked, the tone of his voice revealing how incredulous he thought the idea that Winslow would take that much notice of one of "them."

"They're all called Jose, aren't they?" Winslow said. And they both laughed, although Brewster's laugh was edged with a bit of hysteria.

"So, are you sure?" Winslow said, fingering the vellum envelope. "I've heard that Fenton and Felton are hiring."

"Yes, I'm sure," Brewster responded in a small voice. The mention of Fenton and Felton, a decidedly plebian firm, was pregnant with meaning.

"You'll have to ask for it," Winslow said. "I'll not force it."

"Yes, thank you, sir. I understand," Brewster said. "But you will . . . we can . . . you know, what we agreed on."

"Yes," Winslow whispered sotto voce, his voice laced with exasperation. "If you have a blindfold, you can use it. And I have restraints. If it's easier for you, we can do that if it makes you feel less guilty."

"Light," Winslow said in a louder voice like the flick of a whip. He snapped his fingers as he said it, and the Hispanic attendant materialized from the shadows and lit Winslow's cigar for him. And then he faded away as quietly as he had appeared.

"Well, you'd best be going up," Winslow turned to Brewster and said. "I'll be up shortly. I don't care if the lights are off and you are blindfolded. You are going to enjoy it, so don't look so glum."

"Yes, sir," Brewster muttered in misery. He gulped down his port and moved unsteadily toward the door and to the elevator.

Nice ass, Winslow thought, as he watched the young man move away. Good looker, nicely muscled and trim. Just the way I like 'em. And young men of his pedigree are hard to come by. As only America can produce through generations of residence.

Winslow closed his eyes and let his head loll back into the enfolding supple leather of the Chippendale chair and dreamed of fucking the very presentable and finely familied William Brewster. A year's campaign but all worth it. After a brief reverie of the images of taking the young man from several positions, Winslow realized his cigar had gone out. He snapped his fingers.

"Light."

Nothing happened. Winslow's eyes shot open and he looked to his left, where the Hispanic attendant should be standing. No one was there, but Winslow's empty snifter had been cleared away. No servant, though, and Winslow's cigar had gone out.

"Damn wetback," Winslow muttered. "Probably already half way back across the border. Probably an illegal too. The club standards have gone to shit."

He leaned over and smashed the ash end of the cigar in a crystal ashtray, and, while struggling up out of the mothering clutches of the deep armchair, took up the second cigar, put it in his shirt pocket, and reached for the precious vellum envelope.

While waiting for the ancient elevator to clank its way back to the public room floor, he opened the envelope and took the key out.

612, he thought. I didn't know the club even had six floors. Must be in the attic. I wonder who Brewster ticked off at reception when he checked in.

* * * *

Bill Brewster was naked and lying on his belly on the silk sheet covering the double bed in the middle of the club guest bedroom. He lay in the dark, his eyes covered with a blindfold, his eyelids held

88

tightly shut, his breathing ragged, and his body twitching at what was about to happen.

He heard the key in the lock, and he almost whimpered in uncertainty and fear as he sensed more than saw the brief invasion of light from the hallway before the door was clicked shut and the subtle sound of the rustling of shed clothing reached his alert hearing.

This was his future. He'd made a deal with the devil. He'd been told that Winslow was cruel but that he didn't sustain interest. A couple of months, not more, and he'd move on to other quarry. And then Brewster's future would be made. He'd just have to steel himself. His ancestors had taken the risk and grabbed for the gold ring when they'd sailed for the New World on the Mayflower. At least Winslow had the right pedigree. Brewster could still hold his head up after this. Just some pain and private humiliation, and then his future would be made.

Brewster lurched and made a little yipping sound as he felt strong callused hands taking his wrists and tying them together and then forcing them over his head and tying them off at the headboard.

Such strong hands. A little surprising, the strength, but Winslow bragged incessantly about his garden and how he worked it himself. Brewster shivered a bit. Strong hands. Would that mean other strengths as well?

Those callused hands were running all over his body as he lay stretched out on his belly. He was trembling and trying to think of anything else but what was happening—what was happening at last after nearly a year of putting it off. If he'd let Winslow bed him as soon as the employment deal was set, it would be all over now. It would be done and Winslow would probably already have moved on to fresh tail. No use crying over that now. Just bear it. Pretend to be somewhere else altogether.

But pretending to be elsewhere was becoming increasingly difficult. Those hands were tantalizing. No woman had done this to him, had taken the time to put him into a mood. Pleasurable. He had to admit that it was pleasurable. He was beginning to calm down, and he caught himself sighing.

Hands were on his hips, lifting them, signaling that he was to go up on his knees. He started to rise, and a large hand palmed him between the shoulder blades and showed that only his hips were to go up, that his chest and cheek were to stay flat on the sheet. His arms, trapped above his head were beginning to go numb and to tingle. But the skin of the small of his back and his butt cheeks was tingling too. This was a different tingle, though, brought about by the movement of lips and tongue on his body.

Brewster moaned as a hand came between his spread thighs and took possession of his dick. He hadn't realized it, but he was hard. A flash of embarrassment shot through him. Winslow's attentions had made him go hard. Letting yourself be fucked by a man was one thing, but your body showing that it was enjoying the attention was quite another. He gulped and whimpered as the stroking began. Then he didn't quite manage to swallow a yelp when the bulb of his dick felt the lips open over it. A tongue was flicking his piss slit as the lips slid farther over his throbbing dick. Fingers were probing his balls and pulling on his sacks. Brewster let a deep moan escape his lips.

He was supremely embarrassed, but he couldn't help himself. It had seemed like an eternity of sucking, but it had been mere minutes before he creamed himself from the close attention paid to his dick.

His knees were trembling, and he couldn't feel his arms at all, but he certainly could feel the pounding of his heart against the bed sheet.

Brewster twitched and he gulped hard as the lips and tongues moved from his spent dick and started to rim his ass. He was moving to the rhythm of the attention he was receiving. His chest was sliding back and forth on the sheet and he was slowly rotating his hips back and forth as his hole was being loosened and softened. He groaned and moaned.

The trembling in his thighs increased as he felt the cool lubricant of the probing fingers that replaced the lips and tongue at his rim. He was being forced open by those fingers, which worked their way deeper and deeper, stretching him, preparing him.

He was panting and moaning, his attention so focused on those probing fingers, that he only barely heard the hoarse whisper.

"What?" he whimpered.

"Do you have something to ask?" The voice was deep, throaty. Very quiet, but intense.

"What?"

"Ask me for it."

"What? Oh. Please, yes, please."

"Please what?"

"Please . . . do . . . it . . . Ohh!" The nub of a forefinger had planted itself solidly on Brewster's prostate and he felt like he was going to jack off again, although he was just beginning to recover a hard on.

"Do what?" the voice hissed.

"Fuck me. Fuck me. Oh, please do it. Nowww!"

He had been prepared so slowly and methodically that he was completely caught by surprise at the swift brutality with which the fingers disappeared and big hands grabbed him by the hips and a thick, hard cock thrust inside him.

Brewster cried out, and groaned and begged and writhed under the firm grip of the furious assault. His crying for relief seemed only to excite his master, who pumped hard and dug deep. Brewster had no idea that Winslow had such strength and length and width and stamina in him.

It seemed to go on forever. When Brewster's knees could take it no longer and he collapsed fully on the sheet, his rider followed him, stretched full length on top of him and sucked on his neck as he thrust and thrust and thrust inside him.

Brewster was totally exhausted after his master's spouting and drifting off into a semiconscious state when he felt the restraints being loosened at the head of the bed and his wrists unbound, and he didn't stir again until well past dawn. And, of course, he awoke finally to an otherwise empty room.

* * * *

Room Number 612 did, indeed, seem to be in the hotel's attic, Edward Winslow observed, as he exited the elevator and moved down the dimly lit hallway. And it definitely was in need of redecoration. Winslow had no idea that the FGCC had permitted its guest floors to go so seedy. He'd have to talk to the steward, Richard Warren, about this.

After looking both ways down the hall to ensure he wasn't being observed, Winslow turned the key to room 612, slipped inside, and shut the door behind him with a quiet click. He stood there inside the door, in the darkness, waiting for his eyes to adjust. He was breathing heavily, and his cock was already stirring, in anticipation of what he had campaigned for for nearly a year. He could hear the nervous breathing of his prey as well. Brewster had wanted to be taken while bound and blindfolded to assuage the guilt, but Winslow had been more than happy with this plan. Brewster's nervousness and fear fed the rising of Winslow's cock. He loved to dominate—in everything. That Bill had such a nice ass. Winslow could hardly wait.

His eyes were beginning to adjust. He could make out the outline of the bed and of a wooden arm chair off to the side. He extracted the leather restraints from his jacket pocket and took a step toward the bed.

"Ooff." He hadn't seen the fist coming at him from out of the darkness. It hit him midsection and sent him, doubled up on the threadbare carpeting on the floor. He was immobilized by the surprise and the pain in his midsection.

He didn't manage to even begin to struggle as he was stripped of his dinner jacket and lifted and thrown into the wooden arm chair, which rocked dangerously backward, kept from crashing back only by the hulking figure who had moved to behind the chair.

Winslow's arms were brutally jerked to behind the chair, and he heard the handcuffs snapping together. His own leather restraints were used to bind his chest to the chair back. And Winslow had only begun to regain his breath and presence of mind—to let out a scream of indignation—when tape was slapped over his mouth. Then he was blindfolded and totally under control.

The door clicked shut and he was alone. He was alone, bound to the chair, for hours, it seemed. Winslow seethed the whole time.

What the fuck was Brewster up to? He couldn't just leave him here. The maids would be by in the morning and let him loose, and then he'd ream Brewster to within an inch of his life. So, he didn't want to be fucked. He would regret it. His future was toast. He might have cleared out before Winslow got free, but he'd pursue the bastard to the ends of the earth and make his life miserable. He'd ruin the fucker. He'd find a way to fuck him and then to ruin him.

Winslow had nearly nodded off, his inability to put his hundred-ways punishment of William Brewster into immediate effect, worn down by his spewing of bile within the restraints of the tape over his mouth, when he heard the door click open again.

He heard the movement in the room. The rustling of clothes. Then he felt the hands at his belt buckle. He struggled against the restraints as his pants were unzipped. His head snapped to the side as he was backhanded on the right cheek. And while he was immobilized, stunned by that, he felt his trousers and briefs being stripped off. His butt cheeks were cold against the wood of the chair bottom.

Winslow felt the cigar being taken out of his shirt pocket, and he barely had time to wonder about that before strong arms grabbed him under his knees, pulled his back down the chair slats, spread his legs, and hooked them over the arms of the chair.

Something cold was at his asshole, which puckered right up at the sudden attention it was getting.

The cigar. He was being probed by the Casa Blanca Jeroboam! God, what a sacrilege. The waste of an expensive cigar.

His ass was being worked well, though, and Winslow found himself moaning and groaning behind the taped mouth. That Brewster. What an actor, pretending that this frightened him. Winslow felt himself go harder than he ever had done before. This wasn't so bad.

The cigar was withdrawn and strong hands were under his knees again, lifting his hips up even farther out the chair. He heard the heavy breathing and the shared strain, as a big, thick cock started to work its way into his hole.

Winslow's pelvis was being swung back and forth and to the sides as the cock drove its way up into him. Both of them were huffing and puffing.

Winslow's assessment of Brewster skyrocketed. Boy that young man had balls. Worthy of his Mayflower ancestry. Worthy of being moved up faster at First Families Securities. It had been a risk, but Brewster had played it perfectly. Winslow was loving this fuck.

The fuck went on and on. It was a cruel fuck, an expert taking. Winslow shot off twice during the taking. He felt twenty years younger. This was far better an idea than the one he'd had—although he'd get his shot too.

A true American First Families performance. Pure-blooded American. Deep, thick, complete taking. Yessss!

Winslow was totally exhausted when it was over. He felt the handcuffs snap off and his bounds undone, and he just collapsed back into the chair, trying to pull himself together. When he reached up and pulled the blindfold off, he saw the light of rushing dawn filtering in through the dormer window. He was alone in the room. He painfully, stiffly raised himself from the chair and hobbled over to the cracked porcelain sink in the corner of the room. Using a threadbare washcloth, he cleaned himself as best he could and hobbled back to the chair; picked his briefs, trousers, and jacket off the floor; and put himself back together.

It took him several minutes to smooth out all of the wrinkles, but he wasn't about to walk through the halls of the FGCC without looking exactly like what he was—a pure-blood descendent of the original Mayflower first families of the New World. Pure American down through the centuries. Protectors of all that was patrician Bostonian against the encroaching world of the dirty, impure immigrants.

When he was what he wanted to project, he left the room and went to the elevator. It had been a stupendous gamble on Brewster's part. But it had pleased Winslow. It had been years since he'd come twice in a single fucking. He'd be fucking Brewster, of course, but he had a whole new respect for the man. He certainly had balls.

Winslow didn't even acknowledge the presence of the Hispanic attendant who proceeded him out of the front entrance and flagged down a taxi for him. But after Winslow stiffly folded himself into the back seat of the cab and had made a sour remark about the immigrants who were driving the service cars those days, the attendant rose to his full height and flipped the departing taxi the bird. Flashing a big grin, he slowly pulled a moist and pungent Casa Blanca Jeroboam cigar out of his shirt pocket, lit it, and walked slowly back into the entrance to the world of the First Gentlemen's Covenant Club.

Whiff of Temptation

by Sabb

I gave up smoking ten years ago, for the second time, after keeping off it for six years from the previous time. And it was worse than hard that second time, and I know I couldn't do it again. Even now my brain still starts craving tobacco whenever I smell the sweet aroma of fresh tobacco, fresh cigarettes. Even the fresh smoke exhaled across a table, more than briefly. Ahhhhhhh yes, I only have to smell really good fresh tobacco, for my body to start whatever the smoking equivalent is of salivating. Slobbering in a lustful urge to . . . inhale.

Uhhum. So I try to avoid places people smoke, and smokers. I am also very sensitive to the smell and taste of stale smoke now, and I can't stick my tongue in the mouth of someone who smokes. And I don't want their stale tar-coated one in mine either.

So, my friends and lovers are now nonsmokers. Which is fine, as it also means that they are healthier, will live and love longer, have more disposable income, and well, lots of other good things that go with being a nonsmoker.

So it was quite a shock and very worrying when I started to get a whiff of the smell of tobacco smoke when I visited them. All of a sudden the heady aroma of really good tobacco was everywhere, and it all started at a party Morris had one night—not a real party, but maybe ten people, some wine and a BBQ under the new pergola in his recently replanted garden.

I had to be at work at 6:00 AM the next morning, so I left the party early just as the evening started to warm up, saying, "Bye" to Neil, Arnold, Morris, Colin, and Dave and the rest of them. Ah well, I've got to make a living. But as I was leaving, a wave of rich tobacco smoke wafted past me, and I was almost knocked over by it. I turned to see who it was, but all I saw was the unfamiliar back of a well-built guy with dark hair and a trail of smoke drifting up from in front of him as he walked out to the garden where the BBQ was. And I was stunned to see Morris, who was also a reformed smoker and was now obsessive about not getting the smell of smoke in his furnishings, rush forward and embrace the new arrival in a gush of half-heard words so that I missed his name.

It wasn't the smell of an ordinary cigarette I knew, but I didn't give it much thought at the time; I was just very surprised he was there and glad to be escaping the seductive aroma.

The next day was Saturday, and after work I stopped by to pick Neil up and take him to the gym. We always worked out together on Saturdays and Tuesdays, and I was surprised not to find him waiting at the door for me. But then again sometimes he worked on the weekends and sometimes I'd find him asleep on his sofa recovering from Friday night. Since the door was wide open, I wandered in and took a bottle of Staminade from his fridge. But there was a strange smell, and as I stood up and opened the bottle, I sniffed, and suddenly I was hit by the smell of that tobacco again. The same one as at Morris's, rich and pungent, and in shock again, I wondered what it was doing there and where Neil was.

Muffled noises drew me further into the house, and I wandered on, the smell of tobacco growing stronger, leading me to Neil's open bedroom door. On the bed I saw, and heard, the reason Neil had forgotten about getting ready for the gym.

Neil was on his knees, and I could see his smooth thighs sitting wide outside another pair of solid muscular thighs coated in a light coat of dark, curly hair. Yes, behind him and pumping his ass was the body of the dark-haired, well-built guy I'd last seen at Morris's, whose hairless muscular butt was clenching and releasing as he pumped my moaning gym buddy's ass.

And the aroma of his cigar circled around me. Because I now knew that was what the smell was—a cigar. Yes, the stranger's thick cigar butt sat on a plate on the bedside chest as its owner fucked my reformed smoker, gym buddy, Neil.

Their moans and grunts had led me there, and Neil was moaning more loudly now and writhing under his attacker, as the guy did same gyrating and shallow stroking inside my mate's channel that had me wishing it was me he had there on the bed. I love a guy who can really work his cock around in my ass and reach every part of it, but that thinking was doing me no good. Because the aroma of the tobacco had me starting to salivate. I had to get out of there fast.

So, I escaped, half hard and filled with the desire for a good fuck. But also afraid—because even in the brief time I had been in Neil's house, I had been starting to yearn for the rich tobacco aroma and had been taking deep breaths to suck it into my lungs, ahhh, and slowly exhaling. I'd had to get out of there. Whatever the hunky dark-haired guy was smoking was like a drug to me.

Outside I took big gulps of fresh air and told myself it was much better, cleaner, sweeter, all that, so much more enjoyable than the smell of tobacco. And I also tried to convince myself that the cigar smoker's butt and thighs and back and other body parts were not doing anything for me. I could not get myself hooked on a smoker.

"And he's Neil's," I told myself firmly.

At the gym I worked out hard, breathed deeply, and complained to Garth how hard it could be to stay off them, even ten years after you had given up cigarettes. He agreed. He'd been there too. So by the time I headed home, I had got my lust for the cigar-smoking stranger and his aromatic cigars out of my system.

"So, did you . . . um, come by yesterday? On your way to the gym?" Neil asked hesitatingly that evening when he called me.

"Yep," I said, "And, yep, I smelt it. The smoke. And I saw what was keeping you too busy to notice the time," I said bluntly. "He's a smoker? Geez, Neil."

"Yeah," he laughed, "Well. Don't sound so stuffy. Sorry, but you know it's been a while and I couldn't turn down a hunky guy who wants to fuck, and, man, that was a great one."

"The guy smokes," I said, "All the time."

"Yeah, well, I can handle it."

"But, Neil," I said in exasperation, "I spent six months listening to you moaning how you were dying for a smoke while you wore patches and had injections and hypnosis."

I had been through more hell than Neil, I was sure. Being a successful "giver upper" I had babied several friends though the drama of giving up smoking.

"He imports them. Luca the Latin hunk. Genuine, hand rolled, Cuban cigars made on the sweaty thighs of testosterone-loaded young Cuban men. And . . . and," he stopped and giggled, then whispered, "And you have no idea, Steve, how many things he can do with a cigar."

Geezus, dream on, Neil, I thought, but he was saying it all with real lust in his voice, whether for the guy or his cigars I had no idea.

"And you know cigars are not as bad for you as cigarettes. Cigars have less nicotine and are organic," Neil added.

"Neil," I shouted down the phone, "Don't you dare."

On Sunday I was having lunch with Arnold and his sister at the Aqua café on the waterfront. Lots of fresh air and great views of the lake, and I had walked down sucking in the joys of summer and thinking about sex. Particularly about solid muscular thighs with a fine coat of black, curly hair and topped by a hair-free pumping butt and imagining a nice seven incher. Sigh. I tried to change the image. This was bad.

Arnold and Lydia were late, and I got a nasty shock when we finished our Thai beef salads. I hadn't smelt it on him as we were outdoors, but suddenly Arnold had to get up and cross the pavement, and I watched in shock as he pulled out a pack of cigarettes and lit one and dragged hard on it. I was stunned.

"But . . . he gave up, years ago," I said, gaping at him.

"Don't talk about it," his sister, Lydia, snapped. "I have already yelled at him, but he's hooked already. It's that bloody Luca he's been dating. God, he's a hunk, but he's got a cigar in his hand the whole time and leaves one behind every time he visits," She said angrily. "But of course one cigar isn't enough, he was a two-pack-a-day man when he gave up, and he's already back on to a pack a day"

"Luca?" I asked. "But, um—" I wasn't quite sure how to tell Lydia that the dark hunk was also fucking Neil. "The guy seems to be a one-man conversion to smoking campaign," I said, frowning.

Arnold had had a lump removed from a lung and given up smoking in a panic. Gone cold turkey. I had never expected him to take smoking up again. He came back to the table looking sheepish, and lunch was spoiled. Lydia and I both glared at him, and he reacted by telling us how good a fucker his new boyfriend was.

There wasn't much I could say to that. I knew he was good. I'd seen him in action. I just shook my head at the end of lunch and said, "If you want to die for a good fuck, Arnold, well, don't expect us to come running with the fruit and sympathy when you are in hospital with lung cancer." I was brutal, I know, but we all knew what his family history—was-his father and two uncles dead of lung cancer, and what his specialist had said.

On Tuesday I went to pick up Neil, and I could smell it— smoke—but it wasn't the rich aroma that came from a hand-rolled Cuban cigar, spun off some nubile youth's sweaty thigh. More like the stale smell of Alpine menthol.

"What? No way. I haven't had a smoke, promise," he said, when I confronted him on it, but he didn't look me in the eye.

I dropped him off afterwards, and he didn't ask me in for a drink like usual. I knew why. He couldn't have a nicotine fix if I was there. I sighed and drove off. Damn Luca, I thought. What was he, some one-man devil's helper? Or perhaps he had been let loose on the gay community by Phillip Morris now that AIDS was waning.

102

That night I dreamed of those bare-butt cheeks and imagined the cigar man pumping my ass amid a haze of smoke and woke up sweating. The guy, Luca, was spoiling my sex life.

Ok. I lusted for him, but the cigars—well, they terrified me, and I had no idea if I could resist him, and them. I certainly couldn't have him without succumbing to the other. Fortunately, he was Arnold's date. Well, supposedly.

On Friday night I went to meet Morris; his other half, Colin; and Neil for dinner in town at Goldbergs'. It was busy as usual, and I was pulling my chair out when I realized that "he" was the guy with his back to me sitting on the other side of Neil. I was looking at the back of him, and the faint smell of fine aromatic tobacco was in the air.

"Shit," I said out loud and moved around the table so that I was opposite him and took the empty chair next to Morris. But as I sat down, I could smell smoke again, stale ordinary cigarette smoke, and it was coming from Morris. I leant closer and sniffed. Yes, it was Morris. I felt the blood drain from my body. God, Morris and Neil and Arnold, and who was next? Me?

No, not me too, I thought. At last I got to see Luca's face, and that was no help at all. What his rear view had promised, his front view delivered. Dark, smoldering eyes, masculine Latin features, and good looks. He flashed a smile at me, all white teeth and big mouth. I hated him.

Shit, I thought silently. Shit.

"How's Arnold?" I demanded, suddenly seeing red and looking directly at Luca.

"Arnold? He was well, last time I saw him."

103

"He's smoking again," I shouted. I wanted my anger to overcome my desire. "He's had a lump removed from a lung. He has a family history of lung cancer, and he should never smoke again." I fixed the hunky Luca with a steely gaze, sending waves of hate at him. Well, attempting too.

"Oh," he said, suddenly looking sad. "No, I didn't know that. But he is an adult; he should know what he can do."

I laughed at that idea. "Ha. I laugh at that idea. What, some hunky Latin with a big cock fucks him to paradise and he's going to act like an adult?" I asked. "And you leave him cigars?"

"You and Arnold," Neil said quietly, looking at Luca, "You are dating Arnold too?"

"Yes, and why not/ I am not monogamous, I am not married to anyone," Luca said waving a hand nonchalantly about.

"That pudgy pale guy?" Neil demanded, slightly less quietly, "You are dating him?" Neil looked stunned, and I could understand why. Neil was the product of good genes and ten years of hard training. He was a superb specimen, and he was fussy about the quality of who got to play with the goods. I'd never quite made the grade, though I had lusted after him badly to begin with.

But I wasn't going to let Neil distract me from venting my anger at Luca. "And how about you behave like an adult. Be an adult and stop encouraging everyone you fuck to smoke," I added, knowing I was ruining the party and feeling like some religious maniac on a soapbox, but also feeling I had a right to be angry.

People in the café were looking our way now. We had been talking rather loudly.

"Fucking and smoking are the great pleasures in my life," Luca replied, his eyes hooded and flashing at me. "I fuck many; young, old, handsome, strong, rich men. Many things about a man attract me. But what I like best is a man who has real passion. True passion is rare," he added seeming to stare at me.

"You fuck many? Old? Rich? Well, fuck you," shouted Neil angrily, standing up so his chair fell back with a loud crash. "Fuck you," he spat at Luca. "Are you coming?" he threw at me, and I knew I should leave. A good-looking guy with a cigar looked at me and I was a wreck, in lust and heat. But at least I wasn't smoking again, and I left with Neil.

When we arrived at his place, Neil dragged me inside. "Here. Here," he said, rushing through the house and throwing an open packet of cigarettes at me, then an unopened pack and matches and a lighter and a bag of butts and ash. "Get rid of them for me. Please."

I threw them in the rubbish bin in the park over the road and came back to find that Neil was waiting for me, panting, with his eyes flashing. "No one has ever done anything for me like you have, Steve," he said. "I mean that. No one. And there is one thing that stops me wanting a cigarette, and I know you wanted it once. So I'm hoping you'll help me give it up again. Will you, Steve? Do you still want it? Say, yes," he begged, holding my hand and looking into my eyes.

I was a bit lost, actually. "Um, of course," I said, though I wasn't sure what he expected me to do.

But then he grabbed my arm and dragged me to his bedroom, and my heart skipped a dozen regular beats to jump about like a hooked fish as I realized he was going to give himself to me. My cock lurched, and I was ripping his T off him before he had even unzipped his jeans. I was rock hard by the time my pants got kicked off and we fell onto the bed together.

"Oh god, you don't know—" I babbled, grabbing his face and slapping my lips to his. His arms were running over me like hot liquid as our tongues fought for dominance and our bodies rubbed against each other in a frenzy of heat trying to merge. Hands reaching for cocks and mouths straining now to reach chests and necks.

Somehow his mouth ended up wrapped around my rod, and I was spreading his cheeks and fingering his butt and sucking his balls.

He rubbed his dick between his belly and my chest in a slow, small fucking motion as I opened his ass with my fingers. Then I gave up his nuts and my tongue reached in to him. Wetting and digging into that tight, puckered opening I was going to plow soon, if he didn't make me come first.

In one natural smooth motion, he gave up my rod and rolled over, and I rolled between his spread thighs and was kneeling back with his butt on my thighs and holding the head of my cock to his hole. I played my cock head around his rim, stroking over it and back, watching it twitch; then I had a finger inside making him gape and pressed my rod in.

"Oh baby," I moaned, as he enclosed my dick inside him. "Oh yes."

The finger came out, and my hand went to stroking his tool as I worked into his ass between his moans and whimpers. I wasn't that long, but I was thick. And I let loose years of pent-up lust and desire in fucking him deep and hard as he begged and encouraged me to take him. He had somehow managed to roll a rubber on me in our frenzy, and my only regret in that first wild joining was that I filled the rubber instead of sending my seed shooting into every part of his being, taking possession of every cell of his body. I milked him as I pumped the last of my cum inside him, joining and merging me to him, watching his cream spout and fall on his chest and face and up the bed.

Then I collapsed over him, totally spent, and we rolled into each other and I cradled his butt in my lap and his back to my chest. I sighed in satisfaction, and realized I wouldn't have minded a cigarette, and shuddered. There must have been some faint smell in the air of his bedroom still that was activating my salivary glands. But the urge died fast as I started to engorge again and played with his filling cock. Yes, fucking was definitely a good distraction.

"So, how long do you think we need to do this to cure you?" I asked him, nuzzling his ear and reaching the point of my tongue inside it.

"Oh years and years, I reckon," He replied.

At work a week later I got a phone call. I picked the phone up smiling, thinking it would be Neil, for the third time, but it wasn't.

"Hi Steve, it's Luca," an incredibly sexy deep voice was saying, "I would really like to meet up with you. To get to know you better, to become friends."

"What? Luca, you smoke," I replied, "And I have a guy in my life," I added, feeling warm at the thought of Neil waiting for me when I got home that night.

"I have given up the cigars. Just for you, Steve. There are so few men of passion and you have passion, Steve. I want to fuck you. Since the day at the café, I have thought of nothing else. That evening I gave them up. So, no cigars for a week. For you I have even done that. That is why I have called only now. So you would know that I am serious in my feelings."

"You have given up smoking" I said, suddenly flushed with surprise that I had had that affect on a hunk like him. And the voice brought back memories of his face and body and those glutes flexing and relaxing and . . .

Neil, I knew. It wouldn't have taken the guy six months to give up smoking if he wasn't a man of fixed habits, and he was now including my favorite ice cream on his shopping list.

But Luca? I mean no one gives up smoking in a couple of hours. Or does he? "For me?" I asked, "You have really given up because of me?"

"Yes for you, Steve. So tonight we meet. Yes? I want your butt in my hands, to spread your cheeks, see your hole twitch for me, your cock grow and throb—"

It was tempting. Listening to Luca, I was tempted.

"Sorry," I said, "But I'm taken." And the truth was that once I had fucked Neil, I was hooked on him. I also have an addictive personality.

But I'll confess that I didn't hang up the phone on Luca. Because I knew that if he tried a bit harder—well, I might just manage to find a good excuse to get home late one evening.

Ring Gauge Power

by habu

I don't know why I was so nervous about this account pitch to the president of the Bull Thorne Financial Services company. The company wouldn't be our biggest client. It was probably because being the stockbroker firm to an accounting firm sort of demanded extra careful handling and recordkeeping. I was fidgeting as Bill Fitch, my senior, and I sat in the reception area, waiting for the company's morning management confab to break up before we met with their president.

"God, this must be the last place on earth that permits smoking in the office, and cigars nonetheless," I whispered to Fitch, straining for some form of conversation that would settle my nerves. "The air in there is getting foggier by the moment."

I could make that observation, because the reception area was divided from the conference room where the management meeting was being held by a full wall of glass.

"Oh, that's just their way of establishing the pecking order— or should I say 'pecker order'?" Fitch whispered back. And then he laughed. The receptionist's head jerked around, and she engaged in a moment of struggle on whether to smile or frown at us, obviously not having fully determined who we were and where we stood in the pecking order of the firm's relationships.

"Excuse me?" I was confused. But it was a good confused. Fitch always spun good yarns, and I needed some attention-diverting mechanisms working for me at this moment.

"Look at the cigars they're smoking," Fitch said. "You can tell who tops who in the pecking order by the cigar they're smoking—the length and ring gauge."

"Ring gauge?" I asked.

"Yeah," the thickness of the cigar.

"You're joking." I said. And I flashed him a smile to let him know I appreciated the yarn no matter how farfetched it was.

"No, really," Fitch said. "See the older guy at the end of the table. That's the firm president, Bull Thorne, himself. Look at his cigar. That's gotta' be at least a Toro, one of the longest and thickest cigars they make. And you can pick out a vice president over there. His cigar is a bit shorter and thinner, and they go down from there. See, the signaling is quite clear."

"You're joking," I repeated. And then I laughed. Most of the tension gone out of me. I silently thanked Fitch for bringing me back to earth. If we got this account, it would be my largest one.

"No, really," Fitch repeated. And then he winked at me and put his nose back into a copy of the *Cigar Aficionado* magazine that he had picked up from the table beside the chairs in the reception area and had been leafing through.

* * * *

Some clients thought the "Bull" in the Bull Thorne Financial Services name related to Wall Street symbols, but those who had known Jim "Bull" Thorne the longest knew he had that nickname because he was reputed to have the longest, thickest dick in Texas. Of course, it could just as well have been an acknowledgment that he also had the biggest pair of balls in Houston, based on the dictatorial and ruthless way he ran his highly successful corporation. Jim Thorne was still ruggedly handsome at fifty, and he surrounded himself with those who were equally ruthless, handsome, and on the make for financial success—at any cost or personal sacrifice.

It was all about control and who controlled who, Thorne always told his subordinates. So, that day three weeks earlier than Bull Thorne was pitched by Bill Fitch and his associate from that stockbroker firm, the gasp that went around the twenty-sixth floor boardroom when the newest vice president, Keith Turner, challenged Thorne's decision on the Mason account, was audible down in the ground-floor lobby. It meant nothing that everyone in the room knew Turner had a good point.

Thorne had closed down the meeting immediately and told Turner he wanted to see him in his office—now.

When Turner arrived at the large, corner office of the corporation president, with its floor-to-ceiling windows on two sides, providing an eagle's view of Texas, Thorne, who was puffing hard on his Rocky Patel Vintage 1992 six-and-a-half-inch long, ring gauge 52 Toro cigar, made Turner stand in front of the mile-wide mahogany desk, while the angry president prowled around him, working himself into a frenzy. Thorne locked the door, came around in front of his desk, carefully lowered his cigar to a large, crystal ash tray, and addressed his subordinate through clinched teeth.

"When I made you a vice president, you said you clearly understood who made the decisions around here—who was in control. Right?"

"Right, Bull. But the Mason account—"

"And do you remember what, exactly, I said at the time that you were to do in terms of loyalty?"

"Umm, no, not exactly. But the Mason—"

"Let me refresh your memory, then. I said, in these exact words, 'Don't fuck with me or I'll fuck you.' Now do you remember?"

"Yes, sir," Turner answered weakly.

"And I've made no secret that I fuck men, have I?"

"No, sir." Turner was turning pale now. He knew what the original of "Bull" in Jim Thorne's name meant.

"And I also said at the time that my statement was a literal one. Do you remember that part too?"

"Yes, sir, but—" Turner was speaking in almost a whisper now.

"Well, you have two choices, Turner. I have to have control and total submission in this office. I've made no secret of that. You can either turn and leave—walk out of your job and this office without so much as a letter of recommendation—or you can give me total control and submission. Which is it?"

A slight pause, and then Turner whispered, "Submission. I will totally submit."

"And you will do so in a way you'll never forget," Thorne said with a sneer.

The Bull was suddenly on the move. "Strip," he commanded.

"But, sir—"

"Strip all the way down, move to the center of the room, and throw your clothes over there." While Turner was complying with a sigh of resignation, Thorne was searching around in his drawer for that tube of lubricant he always kept there. Then, with Turner watching him, his lips trembling and letting out a low moan at the sight of what was between the Bull's thighs, Thorne stripped down as well. He walked over to the pile of Turner's clothes and pulled out the younger man's expensive silk tie, and then he walked back to Turner, tie and lubricant in hand.

"Down on your knees and open your mouth to me," Thorne said.

With a sigh, Turner did so, and reached for that gigantic cock, already mesmerized by it.

"No," Thorne said. "I just said to open to me, not to show any signs of control. Hold perfectly still. And raise your wrists to me."

Thorne used that expensive tie to bind the younger man's wrists behind his back. Thorne then pushed his cock into Turner's mouth with one hand and took his head with both of hands.

"A lesson of control," the company president said. "I control everything. You control nothing. All you are is a warm, wet chamber for my cock. Just be warm and wet and open to me. Leave the rest of the control to me."

And although Turner couldn't help gagging a bit, he tried to comply fully with his boss.

"Now go tighter. Touch me closely on all sides." That wasn't at all hard to do, because Thorne was so thick and long, even though he hadn't hardened out yet. Thorne pumped Turner's head back and forth on his cock for a few minutes, trying to demonstrate his demand for obedience, which was total, and getting Thorne's cock real hard.

Then, pulling out of Turner's mouth, the Bull said, "Go down on your back right here." Turner rolled back onto his butt and then on his back without comment or objection. The athletic Thorne went down on his knees between Turner's thighs and pulled the younger man's butt up on his thighs. He also brought Turner's hands over his head and back to his front.

"Now, I'm going to fuck you—unless you've decided you don't want to work for me anymore."

Silence, filled only by the sound of lubricant slapping against tender asshole.

"Good. Now, as I work my way in, I want you to jerk yourself off. And I want you to cum when I'm in to the hilt—and not before. Understand?"

Turner nodded, a serious look on his face. Thorne slathered his dick with lube, guided it to Turner's asshole, and rotated it around, working it in, while Turner began to stroke himself and to pull at his balls with his bound hands. Turner was concentrating hard on how he was going to ejaculate on cue. Thorne was pleased. Turner hadn't questioned the instruction. Turner had been a prime pick for vice president—and, truth be known, Thorne had been planning to pork his young associate for some time—so it was good that Turner was going to submit and be staying with the firm.

Thorne slowly worked his monster cock into his subordinate's ass, as the younger man obediently pulled on his cock. The Bull closely watched the tension build in the man he was fucking and managed to be at seven inches inside him when he yelled "Now" in a raspy voice, and Turner shot his load up Thorne's flat belly. As Turner ejaculated on cue, Thorne pushed his dick in the last half inch. He looked down at the white globs of semen running down his black belly hair and perched on top of Turner's golden-red pubic hairs. He liked what he saw, but this hadn't been enough of a turn-on for the Bull. The display of his control was turning Thorne on, but he needed the closeness the merging of bodies, his fully dominant over the other, before he himself could reach an orgasm.

"You realize this was just for instruction, don't you?" Thorne spoke to Turner as he squeezed Turner's balls and pulled on his spent cock, his own cock still hard and buried to the root in his subordinate's ass. "I was the one who controlled when you had fulfilled this task, not you. Even though you thought this was your responsibility. It wasn't. You realize that now, don't you? You realize that I held off filling you until you had cum."

"Yes, Sir." Turner answered meekly.

"And you know now that this isn't all that I want, don't you? How quickly can you learn? Quick enough to save that vice president's salary of yours?"

"I can learn quickly, sir," Turner answered quietly. "I want you inside me. And I know that you want closeness, tightness as well as submission and control. Is that right?"

"Yes, that's right. I'm going to unbind you now, and I'm going to fuck your lights out right here and in this position, and I want you to show that you can handle the tightness and closeness without the bonds. You will know if and when you succeed because your insides will be bathed in my cum. Do you want that?"

"Oh yes, please, sir. Flood me with your cum."

115

Thorne untied Turner then and enfolded him in his arms, belly to belly and nipples to nipples. Turner's curly red chest hair tickled Thorne's hulking pecs. The Bull wrapped his arms around the younger tightly, holding his back down on the floor. Turner returned the hug, wrapping his arms around his boss as well and holding him tightly, almost taking the breath out of the older man with his strong arms. Turner's strong, swimmers legs wrapped around Thorne below his buttocks, pulling him in close, holding him tight and tightening his ass canal as much as he could around Thorne's already-buried cock.

The two executives kissed deeply, and then Turner buried his face in Thorne's neck, trying to pull himself into Thorne at every point as much as he could. Turner was surrendering to Thorne entirely, and the older man felt the sexual urge flood into him. He pumped and pumped and pumped at various levels, sometimes pulling out to give Turner's prostate attention. The younger man moaned and trembled at this but continued to hang on to his boss as tightly as he could.

When the Bull came, flooding the very center of the younger man in spasms of semen, Turner ejaculated again himself and collapsed back on the rug, arms and legs askew.

"Sorry," he murmured. "It was just too much. I couldn't hang on any longer. I've been royally fucked. This is the greatest."

"Do you want me to pull out of you now?" Thorne asked.

"Whatever you want," Turner answered quietly. "You are in total control. Do what you want with me."

"Good choice," the Bull answered gruffly. "Remember, if you fuck with me again, I'll fuck you again. And maybe I will even if you don't fuck with me."

* * * *

Keith Turner wasn't all that displeased when he was released from the Bull's office. His ass was sore from the gigantic tool the Bull had, but this had answered a question he'd had since he'd come on board and heard rumors that the boss was horse hung. Yes, he could take almost eight inches of thick cock. He'd had that extension toy in his own desk for weeks, wondering if he could get one of his fuck buddies to try out that length, but now he wouldn't have to experiment with that.

He felt slightly humiliated at having had to give up control like that, though, so he was loaded for bear when he saw the memo on his desk from his own accounting section disallowing that bar tab he'd run up at the convention in Las Vegas the previous month. As his rage was building, he opened the center drawer of his desk and pulled out a Don Diego six-inch, 42 ring gauge Londsdale cigar and started chewing it absentmindedly without lighting it.

Who did this Craig Wilson think he was disallowing whatever tab he, a vice president, chose to charge to the office? Sure, they'd played on the same office football team and had playfully snapped each other with towels in the locker room shower—and Keith had obviously been attracted to the young, studly blond—but, as the Bull said, this office was built on the concept of control and rank, and Craig Wilson would just have to be taught where he ranked in the pecking order.

Turner made Wilson stand in front of his desk at attention while he dressed him down for questioning his authority and then he came right up behind the trembling accountant and yelled in his ear, Marine sergeant style, "I was just talking with Bull Thorne today, and you know what he said about insubordination like yours?"

117

"No, sir," Wilson squeaked. "What did he say, sir?"

"He said that anyone who fucked with authority around here would be fucked—literally. Now what do you think about that, Craig?"

"Well, I don't know what to—" Wilson stammered. And then he squeaked again as Turner grabbed him on the ass and squeezed.

"Do you like your job and your generous paycheck, Craig?"

"Yes, sir," Wilson answered.

"And would you do anything to keep them, Craig?"

"Uhh . . . Yes, sir," Wilson answered again.

"Well, you have two choices then. You can walk out of that door and clean out your desk, or you can take a lesson in control and a good fuck. Which is it?"

Wilson smiled broadly and answered. "I thought you'd never ask, Keith."

This didn't please Turner all that much. This wasn't asserting control over his subordinate.

"Come here," Turner said gruffly, and he literally pulled Wilson around the desk to where he stood between the desk and Turner's chair.

"Assume the position and strip," Turner commanded, as his eyes darted around the room. They lit on the window blind cords. Turner went over and jerked a couple of them down, causing the blinds to accordion down to the floor with a crash. As soon as Wilson had stripped, Turner tied his wrists with one end of the cord, a cord for each wrist, pulled the cords through the kneehole of the desk, crossed them, and the tied the other end tight above Wilson's knees, pulling the cords taunt so that Wilson was spread-eagled with his belly flat on the top of the desk and securely held in place. Turner ripped

Wilson's belt out of his pant loops then and fashioned it around Wilson's neck like a dog leash.

Wilson was totally trussed up now. Turner had physical control. Total control. Wilson wasn't laughing now. Wilson needed to be taught the same lesson Turner had endured under the attention of the Bull's big cock earlier today. But Turner didn't have the length and thickness of Thorne. Or didn't he? Turner reached down and opened the bottom drawer of his desk and buried his hand under a pile of papers. He came up with a leather, studded penis sheath with a three-inch extension capped with an extra large stud-covered bulb he'd bought and had been building up the courage to use.

Turner did some lip and spit and finger work on Wilson's ass as the accountant moaned softly for him. After he was satisfied that he'd opened Wilson up sufficiently, Turner sheathed his cock with the oversized studded harness and positioned himself behind the fully trussed figure. Turner palmed the rounded butt cheeks and pushed his sheathed cock up to the opening of the puckered, lubricant-slathered hole with its circle of curly blond hair. Wilson moaned and groaned.

"Oh, shit. Oh, God, no, nooooo!" he muttered, as Turner rotated the studded sheath head around his ass shunt, relentlessly working it farther into the hole.

"The only way you are going to continue working here under me is by submitting totally to me," Turner said. "Do you submit?"

No answer. Perhaps Craig still seemed to think that since they were buddies on the football field, they somehow were on equal footing.

With a push, Turner had worked the sheath extension and two inches of his own cock into the asshole. Thorne's nearly eight incher had little length on Turner under these circumstances, and the extension made Turner's tool, if anything, thicker than Thorne's natural girth.

Wilson cried out. "Yes, OK, I submit!"

"That sounds good, but I don't believe for a minute that you believe it yet." Turner had no idea if this was true; he was just having too much fun skewering the young blond to end this yet.

Turner was in a good five, very thick inches now. The accountant was trembling under his boss and moaning for him to stop, that he was being split. Several more inches in and he was beginning to really feel those studs. Turner took the unburied part of his dick in his hand and rotated it around in Wilson's canal, coaxing him to open more. He was crying and moaning now. The laughter was far behind him.

He kept screaming that he submitted, that Turner had won, and Turner kept creeping up his canal, trying to wipe out his own humiliation earlier in the day, until only about two inches of Turner's cock root were outside the young blond. With the extension, Turner's rod was in a good eight inches now.

"How? How can I convince you I submit?" he whimpered.

"I'll feel it in your body," Turner answered. "When you've totally submitted, all of the tension will go out of your body, and you'll stop yelling at me. You'll take it silently. You'll be totally mine. And then I'll encase your body with mine, and we'll be one. The submissive you and the dominant me. Only then can you work here with me and be my accountant and an acceptable bottom to my top."

"OK, OK, I'll try," he whimpered. "I want to be here. I want your cock inside me. I submit. Totally."

And Turner did, indeed, feel the tension slowly leaving Wilson's body, and he went silent, except for a few grunts and groans he couldn't suppress, while Turner pushed the last two inches of leather- and stud-augmented penis into the accountant's tightened asshole. He left it in there, all the way in, for several minutes, as he felt the tension and fight draining out of the young accountant—and then Turner rode his ass hard and long.

"Oh, God, yessss," Wilson was whimpering. "Fuck me. Fuck me deep. Like that. Yessss. Don't stop." And Turner didn't stop, at least for several minutes. A few minutes after Wilson had spilled his seed on the carpet behind his boss's desk, Turner shot his load into him.

* * * *

Craig Wilson had enjoyed the session in Keith Turner's office, but he hadn't much cared to have been shown so graphically where he stood in the pecking order in this office. It was just the misfortune of the file clerk, Alphonse Pointer, a saucy young black man of pretty Jamaican features, that he chose to give a flippant reply to one of Craig's instructions later that afternoon. Wilson had just stood up from his desk, crushed the Garcia Y Vega five-and-a-half, 34 ring gauge Panatela cigar he had been smoking in an ash tray, taken Alphonse by the scruff of his collar, and pushed him out a door onto the twelfth-floor landing of a disused stairwell shaft. Alphonse had been swinging his hips and tossing suggestive glances at Craig for weeks, so Craig had little question what Alphonse would take from him. But he doubted Alphonse expected the mating dance to be ended so abruptly as this.

Listen you little queen, Wilson exploded once the two were out on the landing. You work for me, see. So, you don't talk back to me.

"Uh, what's . . .?" Alphonse spouted, trying to wriggle out of Wilson's powerful grip.

"Listen, you've worked here long enough to know the office motto, haven't you?" Wilson continued.

"Uhh, I'm not—"

"It's fuck with me and you get fucked." Wilson blustered through gritted teeth. He was going to assert some of his own control in this corporation now. He had a certain amount of rank too. Wilson pushed the file clerk down two more flights of stairs, to the level of a floor that was waiting to be refitted and thus where no one worked now.

"Stop and face the banister," Wilson barked.

Alphonse did so without question, fully cowed by this crazed—but delicious—blond stud from accounting.

Wilson came up close behind Alphonse, unzipped his fly, and pulled out a respectably sized cock. The accountant then doubled the young file clerk over at the waist on the banister with one hand, so that he was facing down the well from the tenth floor, and worked up his unsheathed cock with the other hand, spitting a few times on his hand to lubricate his tool. When Wilson was satisfied he was at least half hard and able to penetrate the younger man, he pulled Alphonse's pants and briefs down off his buttocks, pushed the clerk's legs out to open him up as much as possible under these circumstances, and pushed his dick into Alphonse's gaping, well-used hole.

Alphonse grunted and gritted his teeth as the angry accountant entered him, but he grabbed down for the banister slats with white-knuckled fists and took the blond stud without squeal or objection.

Once in, Wilson tightened the young man up by getting Alphonse's legs between his own. He draped his chest over the smaller man's back so that they were both folded at the waist over the banister and facing down ten flights of stairwells. Wilson latched onto one of Alphonse's ear lobes with his teeth and held on gently.

Wilson could feel the file clerk grunting and groaning, and then sighing and moaning in ecstasy as the accountant's cock lengthened and thickened inside him and filled him to capacity.

"Who's the boss?" Wilson breathed into the younger man's ear.

"You're the boss," Alphonse answered.

"Who backtalks me?"

"Not me, Boss."

As Wilson filled Alphonse to the end and started to pump, the accountant took one of his fists and pushed down the front of the file clerk's pants and the two stroked Alphonse off together, the file clerk's hand under the accountant's, encasing his cock, while Wilson controlled the stroking. As Wilson sensed he was coming, he let loose of Alphonse's earlobe with his teeth and started tongue-fucking his ear. Alphonse held his head closer to Wilson's tongue, loving the sensation. Once more the two managed to come almost simultaneously, the accountant deep inside the file clerk and the file clerk down those ten floors of stair well.

"Wow," was all the clerk said when it was over.

"Yes, wow," Wilson responded. "Now, how do you feel about needing control?"

"I love being controlled by you, Boss. Yes, I certainly do, and you can control me anytime you want. But who can I control in this big corporation? Does the cum stop here?"

Wilson gave a low laugh. "There's always someone you can control in the pecker order, Alphonse. You might try that Cuban body builder in the mail room. You outrank him here."

The file clerk was contemplating doing just that as he left the stairwell. He went down to the cafeteria and poured himself a cup of coffee and then sat down in the smoking section and lit up a three and five-eighth's-inch, 22 ring gauge Exquisito cigarello and schemed about how he could find the mail clerk alone for a thirty-minute pecking order session.

* * * *

The meeting in the smoke-filled conference room was still in full swing and everyone in there seemed to be quite animated on some point or other. All except the firm's president, Bull Thorne. He was looking out toward the reception room, his teeth firmly chomped down on his Rocky Patel Vintage 1992 cigar, and his eyes looking hard and yet dreamy, sort of lustful.

I nudged Fitch. "Why is he eyeing us like that?" I asked. His gaze looked a little too intimate to me.

Fitch laughed. "He's not looking at us; he's looking at the Hispanic mail clerk over at the receptionist's desk—the guy who fucks him."

"The hell you say?" I blurted out. The receptionist gave me the evil eye and I subsided into a hurried whisper. "Why do you say that? You're joking."

"No, I'm not joking," Fitch said. Then he laughed and pointed. "It's all in the signaling. Look at what the mail clerk is smoking."

"What? What do you mean what he's smoking."

"His cigar tops the one Thorne's chewing on. If I'm not mistaken, he's smoking a Flor de Oliva Giant eight-inch, 60 ring gauge Presidente cigar—look, just like this one in the magazine." Fitch waved the copy of the *Cigar Aficionado* magazine under my nose, and he had his index finger pointed at a cigar that, indeed, looked exactly like the gigantic wad of tobacco hanging out of the mail clerk's mouth.

"And you know what having a bigger cigar means," Fitch said. And then he laughed again.

"You're joking," I repeat.

And maybe Fitch really was joking. But the thought that the mail clerk topped the firm president in the firm pecker order loosened me up so that I no longer felt the least bit nervous about pitching Thorne when we got to meet him.

Gotta' hand it to Fitch. He really knew how to reduce the tension in the room. I turned to thank him, as he started to pull a cigar out of his jacket pocket and gave me a very strange and friendly look.

5,000 Words by 5 PM

by Sabb

Ranklestein chomped on his cigar and sucked smoke into his lungs as he stared at the text on the laptop. "Fuck. What a boring piece of . . . of boring crap."

The buzzing of the phone jerked him away. "Hi," he barked.

"Hi. So how's it going? I need those five thou by this afternoon, Rank. Five thousand, is that so hard?"

"Hard? Hard? This Manissus is a moaner and a wimp with the sex appeal of two-day-old roadkill. Geez. I mean, who created this guy? You think I can work miracles in four hours?"

"It was Guy Royal's last heroic, erotic, action fantasy, OK? He was dying of pancreatic cancer, the most painful, Rank, baby, hear that? And his agent had just run off with his boyfriend, and he was almost destitute, for god sake. If it hadn't been for guys like Brad, he'd have . . .ugh, well . . . he'd have starved. And you expect him to be cheerful? Feeling sexy? Hey, get real. Anyway, Guy Royal was a star. A cult figure. *Battle of the Gods* will sell whatever kind of shit it is. You, I am paying to make it raunchy without making it unrecognizable, OK? Fifty thousand sexed-up words by the end of the month, but I need those five thou today, baby."

"Geez, Sol. If I didn't have alimony to pay, I'd say go fuck yourself."

"See. I knew you could do it, baby. So, by 5:00 PM? OK?"

"OK. Ok, all right," Ranklestein barked and slammed down the phone.

"Shit," he added, chomping down grimly on his cigar and returning to reading the first chapter of *Battle of the Gods*. The gay epic that had been recovered from the late Guy Royal's hard drive after his death. A miracle, everyone was calling it. "Another tidy earner they can all live off for a few years till they find another Royal," Rank grumbled, "Christ. I wish they'd buried it with him."

He was reading again.

Fortunately for the man Manissus, the moon was nearly full, and even more fortunately, the goddess' bright silver face was sitting almost directly overhead in a clear night sky. A sky that was typical in that year of dry weather that had been frustrating the regions farmers throughout the mild winter, and looked like continuing into the approaching spring.

The brightness of the night was a fortunate gift from the goddess, because otherwise Manissus would have fallen often as he made his way drunkenly through the narrow unevenly paved streets of the city.

Unfortunately, as far as Rank was concerned, the story was no gift from anyone and continued in the same woefully depressing, long-winded way for quite a few pages before there was even a hint of sword action of either the violent kind or the male/male sex kind.

"Moan, moan. Christ, if he didn't get any, then whose fault was it?" Rank asked out loud as he read on in exasperation, seeing all the missed opportunities for hot action.

It had been far from the intimate evening Manissus had hoped for and needed. Instead, Thesis seemed to have invited all the men of his family along to the dinner party, and it had already been far too late when the last of them had departed. Manissus should have left then himself, but he had waited impatiently all evening to be alone with his friend. Then, when he was the only one left, Manissus had finally staggered over to join Thesis on his couch, believing that the evening would be worth it after all. But Thesis had sat up just as he reached him, wished Manissus a safe journey home, and made his excuses.

"A hunky Greek from the time of the Trojan wars, and all he could do was stagger over and whine when he didn't get any. Geez. I mean, just throw this guy Thesis back on his couch and take his dick in your mouth, and he'd be begging for it after thirty seconds. Guaranteed," Rank shouted as he pulled his own cock free of his pants and gave it a stroke, imagining the two ancient Greeks dropping their linen whatevers and getting naked together on the couch. "Or an orgy. Yeah, the whole damned lot of them. All those relatives he invited along. Oh yeah," a hard-on always helped him think of sex to put in a story. "Hey Brad," he called out between pants. "Come out here."

His houseboy, Brad, padded out to the poolside patio wearing nothing but a thong and an all-over tan.

"Yes? You called, master?" Brad joked, striking a hand-on-hip pose and making his abs bunch up and his arms and legs flex, a blond, bronzed god with the oversized swimming pool in the background.

Now, there was a real Greek god, thought Rank. "Oh yeah, you look so good. But I've got a problem, babe. I need inspiration; I need somewhere to start with this Guy Royal thing. Forget hot sex even. I need anything. It's dead. Like buried." He stuck his cigar back in his mouth and sucked briefly, while taking in what Brad had to offer and stroking himself a bit more quickly.

"I mean this guy is such a bore. You have read this. So, give me inspiration."

Brad frowned. "I liked it; I thought it was very literary, very artistic."

"Literary? Royal wasn't about literary, babe. Royal's all about sword action. Both kinds. I like the café bit, when he sees the hot young guy his ex-buddy Thesis is drooling all over now."

"That bit? That's hot?" Brad asked pouting. "He discovers his buddy, the man he loves is chasing some eighteen-year-old, it's a pivotal emotional moment," he argued.

It was Rank's turn to frown. "Yeah? Pivotal?" he shrugged. "Well, I could see real potential there. Great three-way building. But it's way into the story. There's potential before that. And Sol wants the first five thousand words by 5:00 PM, and hot."

"You'll come up with something," Brad replied huffily, then moved in behind Rank and rubbed his crotch against Rank's upper back, making his employer close his eyes and his head flop about from side to side as he emitted small moans. "Just as long as you don't change the story," Brad said firmly.

"Yeah, the story's got lots of possibilities. Oh, yeah, now that's inspiring," Rank murmured, as he grabbed Brad's arm and pulled him around so he could tug off the thong and wrap a hand around the sausage it had been trying to hide. Brad bent over and they kissed, as the houseboy's hand joined his employer's on Rank's rock hard very thick, six-and-a-quarter-incher.

"Start with yourself, baby," Brad said as he kicked off the thong and pulled Rank's hand free of his stiffening meat. "I'll be back in two shakes," he added reassuringly as he padded back into the low-set, white-painted Spanish-style house.

"OK. So—" Rank returned his attention to his laptop.

Then, when he was the only one left, Manissus had finally staggered over to join Thesis on his couch, believing that the evening would be worth it after all.

"De dah, deh, dah—now—" Rank mumbled and started to type.

Manissus knelt by his friend's couch and grasped Thesis's organ through the fine linen fabric of his short tunic and felt it stiffening instantly. He stroked it lovingly; he had been waiting all evening for Thesis's cock to be rock hard and throbbing. Now he was shaping the fabric around it, feeling it engorging under his attentions, and then, as it grew longer he was licking it, making the fabric transparent—

Brad came padding back with a fistful of condoms and a tube of lube, and Rank looked up at him, "This has potential, loads of it. . . . But, shit, he just lets if drift by. I mean Royal was good. Well, I read him once, and it was real hot and heavy. This . . . this ain't Royal, it's—"

Rank paged forward,

130

. . . a line of men burnt the color of cedar by days spent laboring naked, or almost so, under the hot sun, were passing up and down the two gangplanks running from the ship's side to the new stone dock.

"There's more potential there too," Rank mumbled. "Lines of naked men, sweaty and muscular, I mean . . . when you were visiting Guy, did he ever talk about this *Battle of the Gods*?" Rank asked, frowning and taking a puff on his cigar.

"I think he mentioned something about it. About it being real literature," Brad replied sharply, seeing that Rank had an idea he wasn't going to let go of. "But I don't really remember."

And Rank's thoughts were interrupted just then as Brad's now well-filled tool was pushed at his lips, and he opened automatically to take in and suck his favorite treat.

For several minutes the only noises were Brad's grunts and moans and the sound of Rank's sucking and slobbering on Brad's rock-hard eight inches of cock. Rank always almost choked on it before he got the deep-throating action right, and then it was a smooth head-pumping face fuck that had them both moving on to another plane. And once the action was right, Brad held Rank's head in his hands, guiding it, and as the tension inside him built up, he rolled the middle-aged graying head from side to side as he pushed it back and forth. Brad loved the moving pressure Rank's mouth provided for him, like another kind of all-over stroking action.

Rank's cigar was sitting in the ashtray beside his laptop and went out about the time Brad decided he would come if he kept doing what he was doing. And he didn't want to come just yet. Brad pulled his cock from the sucking mouth with a slurping sound, as Rank tried to hang on to it. He loved sucking cock—loved the feel of a cock in his mouth almost as much as he loved the feel of one inside his ass.

Brad gave him an open-mouthed kiss, playing his tongue about in the warm mouth that tasted slightly of him, and, with his hands under his arms, lifted Rank up. Rank kicked off his own pants and pushed his briefs down and then pulled Brad's hips in tight to his so the two rock-hard cocks were rubbing against each other and sending Rank off into a whimpering sucking of Brad's tongue in his mouth.

Brad pulled free, and Rank cried, "Oh yes, I want your cock, baby, fuc—"

The cry was cut off abruptly as Brad stuffed the dead cigar into Rank's mouth. The loud vocalizing during sex wasn't going down well with their new neighbors, and the police were happy to come and investigate their complaints.

With his mouth now full of cigar, Rank was quiet as Brad turned him around, and Rank chomped down hard on the firmly rolled tobacco as he bent over and rested his elbows on the seat of his chair, stuck his butt up in the air, and widened his stance. He made grunting and mumbling noises as he looked back under his chest, back to what was going on between his spread thighs. His erection bounced up and down, revealing and then hiding his tight balls, and behind him he saw Brad's thighs. Brad moved in closer and inspected Rank's hole and briefly let himself imagine the different ways he could open it up.

He loved giving a good fuck just as much as Rank liked taking one, and his urge today made him stroke over that well-used puckered rim with the big red cap of his own tool, a sight he never tired of seeing. His cock head stroking up and down between the parted cheeks and over Rank's tightly puckered rim.

Rank grunted and moaned and whimpered as he chewed on his cigar before he finally had to reach back for his own dick and stroke himself to completion. He could never hang off like Brad could, and once he felt a cock at his rim, he was usually coming.

Some lube fingered into the slack hole, and Brad was guiding his big cockhead to it. Then, with the head barely in, he thrust hard. The cigar butt shot out of Rank's mouth as he let loose an almighty cry of "Yeeoww." Then he was shouting loud enough to be heard half a block away, as Brad started deep pumping him.

"Fuck. You're fucking killing me. Ohh, I can't take it."

The cigar was too far away to be rescued, so Rank just continued yelling as Brad plowed his ass in a frenzy. The neighbors called the police and were yelling complaints at them at about the same time Rank got hard again. His cries took on a new pitch as he beat himself off and Brad lightly squeezed his balls, and his yell of "I'm coming. Coming, coming, coming" was indecipherable. Brad came with a small grunt and did the rotation of his hips that always made him moan it felt so good, and he rotated them again for another jolt.

Brad finally pulled out, satisfied, and Rank eased himself up and back into his seat, and the two men kissed.

"Just as long as you don't change the story," Brad said firmly, before he retrieved his thong and carried it back into the house.

For a moment Rank sat there silently, still spent and mellow, but then he looked at his computer and finally focused. There was silence for a few minutes as Rank read and pondered.

"He didn't write this," Ranklestein suddenly said, sitting bolt upright. "What is Sol baby trying to pull? Guy Royal never wrote this shit. I doubt he ever set eyes on it even." He frowned and skimmed a bit and then called, "Brad, here, baby."

Brad reappeared in a clean thong, carrying a fresh cigar, and wandered over to his employer. "You rang?" he said jokingly as he handed over the cigar.

"You were there in Royal's house. Just about every bloody day. So, Brad, spill. What's the story with this *Battle of the Gods*?" Rank asked, shoving the six inches of cheap machine-rolled tobacco into his mouth. "This ain't Royal's writing, and don't distract me again," he added, as Brad made a grab for his dick and Rank batted his hand away.

"What was that thing you wrote for that creative writing course you did? The thing you never showed me? That was some ancient Greek story, wasn't it?"

Brad looked surprised, "But. . . you never listen to anything I say. All I am to you is a sex object."

"I always hear you," Rank argued. "You're hot as hell, but I listen babe. I swear. And what's wrong with being a sex object, anyway?"

Brad sniffed, Brad pouted, Brad looked Rank in the eye and said reluctantly, "Guy liked it," and, straightening up to his full six feet, he added; "He was going to help me knock it into shape and find a publisher. That's why it was in his computer." Then he crumpled up and his eyes went round. "Are you going to tell Sol?"

Rank didn't even have to think about that. "Fuck Sol. Far as he's concerned, this is Guy Royal's story. And if it's Guy Royal's, it will sell and we all get paid and everyone's happy. This has potential. I can make it raunchy. You didn't put anything else on his computer, did you? Leave any disks around someone could find? Anything like that? I mean Sol's desperate . . . and I can make anything hot—"

"No," replied Brad, huffily, "I slaved over that, Rank, and Guy said it was a work of art, real literature."

"Humph. Guy was dying in poverty, and you were feeding him, babe," Rank replied, patting Brad's ass. "I can tell you it ain't going nowhere as it is. But why no sex, baby? That's all it needs. It's got real potential, so many scenes that can be turned into strokes. So why, baby?"

"Because I wanted to prove that I can do more than just give a great fuck, Rank," Brad replied in anguish.

Now the truth was out Brad was starting to think of arguing for *Battle of the Gods* to be left as it was, unraunchy and literary, but he'd already had ten rejections on it and was getting depressed. And he had some idea of what Guy's books had earned the old man. He was saved from further thinking by the bell, as just then he heard the door chimes and instead of arguing with Rank he went to answer it. He knew who it was, so he greeted the two policemen by throwing the door wide and striking a hand on hip pose for them, his abs bunched up and his muscles flexed and a big smile on his face.

"And what can I do for you today, officers?" he asked.

* * * *

Three months later.

Ranklestein chomped on his cigar and sucked smoke into his lungs. "Fuck. What a boring piece of . . . of boring crap."

The buzzing of the phone jerked him away. "Hi," he barked.

"Hi. So how's it going? How's *Servant of the Great Moghul* going? Another week, Rank. OK?"

"OK. Ok, it's boring shit, but I'm the great Rank. I can make anything raunchy, right, Sol? And how's *Battle of the Gods* selling?"

"Off the shelves, Rank. Still flying off the fucking shelves. Hottest thing Guy ever wrote. One hundred thousand copies local U.S. sales already," Sol replied. "And have you got anything else off those disks Guy gave Brad to keep safe for him?" he added in a wheedling voice.

"I reckon we can make something more out of them, Sol, baby. Couple of story outlines, and a few more disks to go through," Rank replied, leaning back in his chair and sucking contentedly on his cigar. "Yeah. A few more disks. Guy was sure prolific. And I reckon he started twice as many things as he finished, Sol. Yeah. Those disks of Brad's are a veritable gold mine. His lawyer's drawing up that contract, by the way."

"Hey, do we need a contract, Rank. I mean Brad's family," Sol exclaimed.

"Brad's not getting any younger, Sol. He's got to think of his old age. And if he's anyone's family, he's mine, Sol, baby. OK? So, ciao. I gotta go sex-up this crap." Rank cut the call.

Brad was seated on the other side of the patio table bent over his laptop, "So, how many books do you expect me to write?" Brad asked, looking over the top of his reading glasses at Rank. "And one day I want to be taken seriously as a writer, Rank. I'm not pumping out great historical novels for you to raunch up forever, you know," he added, pouting at his business partner.

"Sure, baby. But this will improve your writing. And we can sell however many you can write, baby. So, how's the last chapter of *Servant of the Great Moghul* coming?" Rank asked.

Brad got up, naked except for his thong, and came around behind Rank and rubbed his mound over Rank's back. "You're distracting me, babe," Rank moaned as he put his cigar in the ashtray and turned around and flipped Brad's growing dick out of his thong and made love to it with his tongue. He probed the slit as the big cock hardened up and tasted the precum that the finger he had up Brad's ass was helping to make flow. He had a star to keep happy now, and he loved any excuse to suck cock, so there was no problem.

"Tongue around," Brad groaned and Rank obliged him, his tongue swirling about the head of Brad's cock. Then the cock was moving further into his mouth, moving down his throat and then out again. He gulped and sucked and took it all in again. Feeling the soft cap stroking his throat, the slick hardness and tasting the salty taste. He tried to hang onto the big meaty piece as Brad pulled it free.

"Over," brad ordered and Rank obediently leant over the table and spread his cheeks and wiggled his butt as he widened his feet. "Give it to me. Give it to me, babe," Rank wailed loudly, as Brad dug a finger into his hole and found his prostrate.

Then it was two fingers, and then three stretching Rank's ass, and his groans and shouts got louder, and he couldn't hold back on stroking himself. Brad didn't bother sticking the half smoked cigar in Rank's mouth. He quite enjoyed occasional visits from the local police, and it had been a while. Instead, he used his cock head to rim Ranks ass and then, positioning it at his entrance, drove it in with one great plunge.

"Yeoooooowww," Rank cried as the thick eight-incher buried itself to the hilt inside him.

"You're killing me," he wailed, as Brad bottomed inside him, and his cries kept up as Brad fucked him slowly for a good twenty minutes, before coming, at the same time as Rank let loose his second load of cream.

After they had kissed Rank picked up his cigar and relit it.

"Guy Royal smoked cigars too." Brad observed. "Do you think I'd be taken more seriously as a writer if I smoked a cigar?"

"No," Rank replied sharply, "And stop distracting me. You haven't finished the last chapter, have you, babe? Have you even started it?"

Brad pouted and hearing the front door chimes, hurried off to answer, leaving Rank worrying about his deadline. No, their deadline, Rank realized, sighing and taking a long draw on his cigar.

La Lectura

by habu

"He was an old man who fished alone in a skiff—"

The rich, resonating, calming baritone of La Lectura began to weave Ernest Hemingway's *The Old Man and the Sea* for us for perhaps the hundredth time, as we Torcedores settled once more into the rhythm of preparing our bunches of tobacco leaves perfectly for the press. We could not have done our demanding work without La Lectura, the reader who sat on the dais on the cigar factory floor, reading to us, first from the daily press and then from classical works—and sometimes, to our great privilege, reciting poetry to us in perfect rhythm to the set movements of our leaf bundling.

In this way he was not only transporting us from the onerous work of bunching the leaves of a perfect Vegas Robaina cigar in the demanding style of the Entubado, rolling each of five varieties of tobacco leaves separately and covering them with the binder Capote leaf before sending the bunch to the press, but also in transporting us beyond the drabness of the factory.

Day in and day out, we gathered in the dusty outskirts of Minas de Matahambre in Cuba's Vuelta Abajo region, famous for its premium cigars, at this dimly lit, factory—more a cavernous open-ended shed than a building—to repeat again and again, the perfect

139

bunching of cigars that each would sell on the European market for more than one of us made in two week's time.

La Lectura was salvation for us—and more for me than any of the other workers here. Only he, Estaban, and I were of Spanish stock. All of the other workers here, peasants all, were Mulattos or Mestizos. I had worked among them for nearly two years in almost complete isolation, and not only because of our different statuses. I chose to live not in the village but in a small, crude shack at the seaside, more than an hour's walk from the factory. Isolation was my protection; I had my secret to bear. I lived in fear that the others would find me out and I'd lose even this existence and have to retreat even farther into the island's interior.

I rested for a moment from the work of the Torcedore, the cigar roller, to gaze at Estaban, La Lectura, the glorious alien presence in this room, delivering culture and transport from this world of care in his rich baritone voice.

Estaban paused in his reading, seemingly sensing someone was watching him. I lowered my face, not wanting him to know it was me. But I slanted my gaze and saw Estaban's eyes stop and link with those of Teotilo, the dark-skinned Mulatto, small and somewhat effeminate of stature and slow of wit runner, who took our bunched tobacco packets from our rolling tables to the cigar presses. Teotilo was barely as old as I was, but he had been working here for ten years or more, since he had been a boy of no more than nine or ten. He was a good-looking young man of pleasant humor, despite the drabness of his never-varied, subsistence life. But, like any of us who could not escape this life, his prime would be over before he reached twenty-five, and then, overnight, he would become an old man. In his case, as small-boned and thin and slow-witted as he was, I could not see him living into his thirties. But, then, maybe being a little dense helped him endure this monotony.

He had stopped in the rhythm of his running from factory tables to press and was looking at Estaban in total awe and admiration. Estaban was from Havana, another world altogether from Minas de Matahambre, a paradise, albeit thin veneered, of culture and sophistication and beauty to country peasants who had never been outside their isolated provinces in the remote peninsulas of Cuba. And Estaban was a handsome, well-built man of pure, patrician Spanish stock. This was in addition to being educated and refined and to having that rich baritone voice that had brought him to the highly honored position of La Lectura for one of the best of Cuban cigar brands, the Vegas Robaina, in the heart of the island's tobacco region.

I saw the grin spread across Teotilo's face as he realized that La Lectura had singled him out for attention and a smile. The women rollers near me, Estelle, Maela, and Yelina, all as smitten as Teotilo with the handsome, mysterious, velvet-voiced La Lectura, sighed at the realization that Estaban's smile was not for them and returned to their leaf bunching.

Teotilo seemed almost to melt on the spot in the sunshine of Estaban's smile, and I almost melted with him. I was so, so lonely among these Mulatto and Mestizo peasants, and so, so bored with the monotonous repetition of the leaf bundling. If it wasn't for Estaban—a Spanish city-formed soul like me—and his rich baritone reading connecting us with and transporting me to the outside world, I could not endure this existence for much longer. I would have given anything if that smile had been for me. But I could not even think of it; it brought me too close to the raw edge of my secret, what had banished me here in the first place.

"Ssst. You are lagging behind, Ramon," hissed Ernesto, the shift foreman, one of those barely thirty-year-old countrymen who had already collapsed in on himself in ugliness and ill health, one foot in the grave, the other foot on this factory floor until the day he no longer could stand.

"Take care of that one," Ernesto continued in a hoarse whisper, nodding his head toward the dais. "He does not belong here and may not be here for long, not if the rumors of what sent him out of Havana are true. Best leave him to the half-wit, if the rumors are true."

And then, leaving me to ponder that and to reach for a leaf of the first variety of tobacco to be rolled and bunched into a perfect Vegas Robaina cigar, Ernesto took two steps along the edge of the factory table and cuffed the runner, Teotilo, roughly on the back of head.

"The presses are waiting, dim-wit," he hissed. "Stop gawking and pick up the rhythm."

With that, La Lectura broke his glance at Teotilo, lifted the book in his hand, and began reading in that rich baritone of his, rhythmically, providing the beat for the preordained, precise, movement-efficient steps of the leaf bunching process.

". . . and he had gone eight-four days now without taking a fish."

Not too many days after that a hurricane brushed past the northwest peninsula of Cuba in the night, appearing without warning in our remote, almost-forgotten Vuelta Abajo region, stripping the

142

trees of their leaves and smaller branches and churning up the gravel and mud in the already deeply pitted paths that hardly classified as roads. I had no means of communication even if the telephone service had withstood the winds. And not knowing how Minas de Matahambre and the cigar factory had fared in the night's storm, I had little option other than to pick my way through the fallen debris for two hours on what was normally a one-hour trek from my seaside shack to the town.

Most of the workers were gathered at the factory when I arrived. The town's electricity was out, and, more seriously, the only roads into the town were impassible. Ernesto informed us there would be no cigar rolling that day. The freshness of Vegas Robainas had to be guaranteed, and there was no guarantee when a shipment could be gotten out of the town and to Havana, so production was just being suspended until more was known on possible scheduling. Ernesto did say that if I wanted the day's pay, I, as the strongest of the workers present, could stay and move bales of tobacco onto pallets in case the stream running next to the factory flooded. I readily agreed to stay, not wanting to miss the pay, such as it was, and having already walked into the town. There was no question that La Lectura would be expected to do such work, and Ernesto dismissed Teotilo with a sniff as being too small to lift the heavy bales and not bright enough anyway to understand where they should go to escape the danger of rising water.

For Ernesto's part, he happily decamped to the café in the town's square with Estelle for a thimble of wine and an unexpected fuck in the café's back room while his wife assumed he was safely hard at work at the cigar factory.

Not long afterward I was moving bales of tobacco into the factory's store room when I heard noises from a dark corner of the shed, behind some tobacco bales. Instinctively, I sauntered over to see what was making the noise and just barely was able to hold myself in check before revealing my presence, just on the other side of a stack of bales from where the two were fucking.

They were both naked, Estaban's finely formed, light-skinned body more easily discernible in the dim light. Teotilo's smaller, squatter dark-skinned body was belly down on a tobacco bale. The balls of his feet were barely able to stretch to the floor, and he was rising and falling on his toes to the rhythm of the thrusts of Estaban's cock between his butt cheeks. Estaban was covering the small Mulatto figure closely from behind, his chest pushing Teotilo's down on the fragrant broad, compacted tobacco leafs at the top of the bale, and his mouth very close to Teotilo's ear. Teotilo's smile at the taking was beatific.

The sound that I had heard and that had brought me to this corner of the shed was the rich baritone murmuring of La Lectura.

He was reciting love poetry to Teotilo as he fucked him. "If I can stop one heart from breaking, I shall not live in vain. If I—," he was whispering in the young peasant's ear. Teotilo certainly didn't recognize the poetry of Emily Dickinson when he heard it, but I, city raised in the family of a prominent doctor, did. But Teotilo obviously didn't care. He was completely transported not only by the fuck but by the overwhelming presence of the cultured and strong-cocked La Lectura. He was being taken into a new world of passion and desire he never before had imagined possible and possibly never again would be able to attain. This was his moment, the sum total of any excitement he would be able to wrest from life was, quite possibly, wrapped up in this fully possessing fuck by a master of lovemaking in the back corner of a cigar factory shed in the remoteness of the Cuban countryside.

And I was transported as well. Standing there, in the shadows, voyeuristically sharing in Teotilo's taking, my hand stroking my own hardened cock through the thin cloth of my trousers, I ached for what Teotilo was receiving. The husky-toned love poetry; the strong, virile body of Estaban encasing mine; the movement of his manhood inside me.

They were kissing, and Estaban was stroking in a strong, steady thrusting. Teotilo was sighing and moaning. I was moaning too, but I didn't really realize I was until Estaban's head turned toward me.

I have no idea whether I retreated farther into the shadows in time, but I sensed that Estaban's gaze had taken me in, possibly not realizing it was me, but surely knowing someone was there. But it didn't seem to matter. Teotilo grunted and groaned at some more intense change in Estaban's fucking, and La Lectura began discoursing again, this time from Shelley, in a stronger voice than before, a voice that clearly carried to me halfway back across the shed to where I had been working and where I, full of envy and jealousy and want, resumed moving bales.

"I bring fresh showers for thirsting flowers, From the seas and the streams; I bear light—"

Not only love poetry, I realized, but poetry that transported the one he was making love to out of this dreary existence. I ached for the attention that Teotilo, the half-wit Mulatto, was being accorded, probably not even half capable of fully appreciating the gift he was receiving.

It did not get back to my shack by the sea until late that evening. I had worked hard all day, trying to purge myself of what La Lectura had awakened in me. Those dangerous secrets, the weakness that had caused me to escape Havana and to seek the isolation and scourge of the hard but honest work in the remote cigar factory. The urges were nearly overwhelming. I wasn't even sure I could return to the factory. Ernesto had been more right than he imagined. La Lectura was a danger to me. I wasn't even sure that my hands could control their trembling in La Lectura's presence and under the influence of his stroking baritone voice enough to be able to go through the demanding movements of the leaf bunching.

I stripped down to my undershorts by the door to my shack and pumped the water up until it rose up the water pipe by the door. I pumped for some time, standing under the cold water sluicing down onto my tired, aching, but yearning body. I dried myself with the towel hanging there and entered the dark single room of my shanty.

The voice was low, rich, husky, mesmerizing. "Shall I compare thee to a summer's day? Thou art more lovely—"

Shakespeare. I had been chilled by the cold water sluicing over my body, but I began to tremble in earnest now, my knees knocking together. My first instinct was to turn and flee, but my feet moved on their own command. They drew me closer to my cot, to the source of the poetry.

"Come to me," La Lectura murmured.

He was reaching out toward me. I felt myself going up on the balls of my feet, wanting to move toward him but holding back.

"You want me, don't you?," he whispered in the rich baritone voice of his. "I could see it in your eyes."

"No." I whimpered. But I found myself shuffling toward the bed.

"No? Could I have been wrong?"

"No." I said again. This time so much weaker. Resolve draining out of me.

"No, what?" The voice. I would melt for the voice alone. But so much more was on offer than the voice.

"No, you weren't wrong," I capitulated in a whisper.

He was on his back on the cot, naked. Beautiful. Fully aroused. Ready for me.

I stood, at his direction, a leg on either side of the cot, over his chest, as his soft mouth came up to my cock and swallowed me and transported me beyond this world. He had lubricant, and while he played my cock with lips and teeth, his fingers opened my canal and prepared me for mounting.

I stood there, whimpering and remembering. Remembering what had sent me into the countryside. Being overwhelmed with the realization of how much I had missed this, how much I wanted it. How much more I wanted it from La Lectura.

When we were both ready, he capped his sword and pulled me down onto the center of him. I cried out as ever before at the initial entry, but the memories flooded in, and my walls luxuriated in the expanding of the throbbing invasion and closed lovingly around his prodigious tool. He was holding me by my hips with his hands, but the balls of my feet knew the rhythm, remembered what to do, how to leverage off the floor on either side of the cot, and I was rising and falling on his manly staff, drawing him ever farther into me.

"I knew it. I knew it would be like this," he murmured, his voice turning dreamy. "I have wanted you since the first moment. I have dreamed thee; I have sought thy essence, to assuage thy sadness. To see thee smile; to smile for me alone, to melt and meld to me and to be mine to the depths of thee."

Not any poetry I'd ever heard, but poetry to me. The words of love I'd longed to hear for a lifetime, that I'd never even heard in Havana.

He had lifted his head to me and he was kissing my nipples and my sternum. His lips went up my chest and into the pit of one of my arms and he was licking and snuffling me in there, inhaling my essence.

"So young, and beautiful and perfectly formed," he was whispering. "And so tight and deep and warm inside. I want to possess you—to the quick, moving as one."

He was stroking my cock with his fist, and I was sighing and moaning for him, lost in his attentions; awed that he was making love to me with his rich voice and his throbbing cock.

When I had cum in a great spouting of pent-up cream, he turned me on my belly on the cot and covered me closely with his body and began a rhythmic stroking of his cock down into me between tightly encased butt cheeks. He was growing larger and my channel was more constricted than before. The full circle of my interior walls felt every vein and tremble of his moving cock. And loved it, remembering, remembering.

I was so fully focused on the waves and waves of pleasure rising up from the center of me that I have no idea when he'd begun reciting again in whispering lips at my ear lobe " . . . Kissing with golden face the meadows green; Gilding pale streams with heavenly alchemy . . ." Surely Shakespeare again.

I melted and drifted off into another, more beautiful world.

I awoke hours later, in his arms, his cock tumescent inside me, spent after multiple takings and flowings in the earlier hours. His breathing was regular, and I didn't realize he was awake.

"You'll come when I call?" I was amazed, flattered that he even phrased it as a question in that rich, possessing voice of his.

"Yes. Anytime, anywhere."

"Here. Now."

I was being lifted onto my knees, and he mounted me astride my hips and was quickly rising inside me again. A hand came around and across my belly, taking possession of my ball sac and the base of my cock. And I was moaning and sighing and being stroked in dulcet tones with snippets of Shakespeare's sonnets as La Lectura, my lover, restored purpose and pleasure to my life. I could sing for joy now as I rolled those perfect Vegas Robaina cigars just as long as La Lectura was there on the dais and in my bed to provide rhythm and poetry to my life.

Independence Day

by Sabb

The fourth of July. It was cold, a late summer, and they said it would be a dry one. There had been snow late in winter. Not that the snow often sat around in the south of England. But Spring had been poor too, and today he wore a light overcoat.

Mike climbed up from Green Park station into a windy Picadilly and sparse, hurrying crowds, his coat tails flapping about his legs. It was Independence Day in America, he thought as he strode along. "Humph." Mike grunted as he always did at the idea of independence on this day. And then he had arrived in Jermyn Street, and wandered into the shop, past the front counters and into the quiet wood-paneled room at the back.

"Ah, Mr. Forte. A windy day, isn't it?" Andrew greeted him. "And three months gone already? My how time flies. And you are keeping well?"

"Yes, fine. And you?"

"Very well, sir. Very well."

"And how's the tobacco business?" Mike asked with a small smile.

"Ah," Andrew sighed, spreading his hands and looking heavenward in resignation. "We manage. But not what it used to be.

150

Not what it was when you and Mr. Jameson first came in, sir. Why then we had—"

"Eight assistants." Mike put in, smiling. "Including old Mr. Grey, who started with Alfred Dunhill just after the Second World War."

"Ah, yes. Old Mr. Grey. Dead for—five years now. But you're here for Mr. Jameson's cigar, sir, and here I am chatting away," Andrew said, suddenly busy.

"Yes. The usual," Mike said. "Two years, exactly," he added, wanting to make a statement, and Andrew shook his head sadly.

Back home Mike put the package aside and poured himself a whiskey from the Johnnie Walker bottle in the drinks cabinet. Then he sat down in his big easy chair by the fire and placed the bag in his lap and sighed. He took a sip of whiskey and set the glass down on the small polished side table before his thick old fingers gently opened the bag and then set that down on the table beside his glass.

He gently lifted the metal tube he had unwrapped and held it between his hands, seeing the shine on the metal, reading the familiar printing on it, feeling the weight of it, the length. A small smile teased around the corners of his mouth, and he closed his eyes for a moment, savoring the anticipation.

Then he lifted the tube to his face and pulled the cap off and held the mouth of the tube to his nose, and as the first burst of rich tobacco aroma escaped, he breathed it in, long and deep, filling his lungs with it. And he closed his eyes, and it all came back to him.

Richard, mature and graying, but still solid and strong. Laughing, his cigar ready, waiting for later. Unwrapped; then set aside on the small side table and the room smelling of it. That rich aroma of really good tobacco. And kissing, the two of them kissing on the sofa, then taking the short walk to the bedroom and slowly undressing each other, taking off each other's pants as they smooched like a pair of young lovers.

Him going down and sucking that familiar tool that he knew a dozen ways to make harder and longer, as Richard groaned and pawed at his head, even when he had lost his hair. His own dick filling at the taste and feel of his lover's. Then being pulled up suddenly and kissed hard. Feeling a firm hand encircling him, pumping and rubbing, teasing in his slit so he burbled and drove his tongue into the cigar taste of Richard's mouth.

Then fucking. Richard liking it long and slow, but deep. Richard grabbing at things, at life, strongly and deeply. Mike always wanting it to be a symphony, a melody of high notes and low notes long and slow, wanting to be played like some musical instrument. And Richard, big and definite, but always doing that when he fucked. Being gentle yet hard, understating how to work his ass so he cried out and moaned for it. And often coming together, knowing each other and working at it. No it hadn't just happened, but they made it happen, most of the time. For twenty-two years.

Mike had unzipped himself, and his dick was filling rapidly under his stroking hand, his fingers playing over his slit the way Richard's used to, his eyes closed, the cigar to his nose. Then he set the cigar aside, and his lungs full of the rich aroma of memories, he leant back and stroked himself as he ran a hand over his chest, pinching his nipples through his shirt and feeling the movement of a hand on his belly as he stroked himself to completion.

He sat there, spent, his dick hanging out, cupped in his hand and slowly going tumescent. His mind hazy with memories of the past. Richard and him lying against each other, cuddling, for a few minutes. Then Richard pulling on a dressing gown and going into the living room and pouring them both a drink and bringing it back to the bedroom with his cigar and only then lighting it, and savoring it as they talked in the warm afterglow. Later maybe watching TV together, or reading. They had never been young together.

Then Mike smiled, and, taking one last whiff of the fresh cigar, he'd found they lost their magic after three months and ritually burned them, he returned it to its tube and, getting up, put it in the cabinet with the drinks and poured himself another one.

"To you, Richard," he said, holding the glass up briefly, knowing that the fourth of July would never be independence day for him. "Wherever you are."

About the Authors

Shabbu is the combined pen name for two established authors, one on the East Coast of the United States and one on the East Coast of Australia, who spin erotica together in cyber space. **Habu,** a bisexual former supersonic spy jet pilot, intelligence agent, and diplomat, is a published mainstream novelist and short story writer under another name and in another dimension of his life. An extensive offering of his erotic e-novels and anthologies is available at eXcessica.com. **Sabb,** once an accountant and sometime property developer, is a wild barbarian at heart, but knows that love is out there of you're lucky enough to find it.

www.BarbarianSpy.com